MW01240830

LOST WATERS

Book 3 in the series: In Defense of Mankind

Written by:
Ron L. Carter and H.R. Carter

Copyright 2022 by Ron L. Carter and H.R. Carter

Published at Smashwords

Smashwords Edition, license notes

Disclaimer

The people and places appearing in this book, as well as the story, are fictitious. Any resemblance to real people, living or dead, is entirely coincidental.

There are real monsters on this Earth and true monsters not of this Earth. Whether we are young or old, we know it to be true. To make this a better world that we live in, we must always be diligent and be in Defense of Mankind.

Table of Contents

Chapter 1 – Home Sweet Home

A light fog hung over the tip of the surrounding mountains as the morning dew dissipated. A crispness filled the air as Zak Thomas stepped onto the open front porch. He had helped his grandfather build the large wood patio during a few free weekends in High School. As he stood there, he temporarily visualized how proud his grandfather was of him for taking the time to spend with him to add the porch to the older 2000-square-foot house. Those were happy and bonding times for him and his grandfather.

Peering across the open area in front of the vast wilderness, he smiled contentiously as he leaned against the porch's post. The feeling was engraved in his face as he felt the safety of the old 40-acre farm. An old wooden fence meandered up and down the smaller slopes, culminating into a circular wooden fence surrounding the home. The grasses on the hill and around the main property stayed short and presented a lush clearing with several small buildings used for farm equipment and ranching supplies. The property was part of the Skokomish wilderness in upper state Washington, where Zak grew up as a child. The ranch lay on the Eastern slope of the ridge that overlooked the small valley and had great views.

His grandfather, John Thomas, owned the farm since the mid-1940s. After his discharge from the US Marine Corps, he farmed and maintained the property. He had spent years fighting the allies' enemies during the second world war. After his release from the service, he picked this farm because of its solitude away from people and neighbors.

Zak had inherited the property when his grandfather died five years earlier but had only recently moved his family here. He moved from his small home on the outskirts of Liliwaup, Washington, in the Olympic basin. Zak, his wife Julie, and his two-year-old son Christopher shared the house and the forty acres. They had only recently moved to the home after Zak and Julie became burdened with questions from people in town and tourists that had heard Zak was known as "The Monster Hunter."

Between Julie's work as a substitute teacher and Zak's monthly army pay, along with the generous signing bonus The Agency gave him from his previous work with them, they lived a comfortable life when he initially came aboard the military team.

Zak did enjoy getting away now and again on light jobs the military sent him on because he could stay statewide during those short trips and accomplish the goal of his quick missions.

Julie walked onto the patio with Christopher on her right hip and a phone in her hand. She stood next to Zak and said, "It's Captain Chuck Hiller, and he wants to talk to you about something he feels is important." Zak rolled his eyes and laughed, "It's always important to Chuck." She handed the phone to Zak and went back inside.

"Hey, Captain Hiller, what's up?" Hiller said, "Old buddy, we have another mission for you. It's one we can't figure out yet. I'm sure you have heard of the Alaskan Triangle and all the weird things that go on there. The Triangle connects Anchorage and Juneau in the south to Utiqiagvik, along the state's north coast. It is some of North America's most rugged, unforgiving wilderness." Zak replied, "Yes, I've read and heard a few things about that area. I know it has miles of wilderness with a lot of unexplored areas. I've also read that sixteen thousand people have disappeared in the area in the last thirty years." Hiller replied, "Yes, that is correct."

He told Zak, "In 1972, a small craft carrying a U.S. House Majority Leader and other members vanished in the Triangle. After months of searching, no plane or bodies were found, not a trace of anything. The Marine Corps sent in a squad of six highly trained soldiers, four men, and two women, to try and locate the downed craft. The squad never returned and disappeared just like the plane they were searching for, and no trace of them." Zak replied, "That does seem strange." Hiller said, "Those mountains have tons of deep snow and ice with many cervices, giant holes, and hidden caves in the ice that people can slip and fall into and never to be heard or seen again. But it's not likely an entire plane and people aboard would completely disappear.

I wouldn't have said this fifteen years ago, but we now know a magnetic anomaly can give rise to a giant counterclockwise space Vortex, and we believe one is in that Alaskan Triangle. Some scientists believe that if caught in one of those vortexes, you can be captured and transported into a wormhole or another dimension, which would be it for you. That could've happened to that plane, the people aboard, and the soldiers searching for them.

Here is one of our problems, Zak. Two weeks ago, four original squad members who searched for the plane and the passengers after it went missing were discovered alive. They were dazed and confused and found in an area of the Ozark Mountains in Arkansas." Zak said, "Wow, that also does seem strange, but only four of the original squad members seem even more puzzling. Being brought back could suggest a Vortex or a portal in the Alaskan Triangle and one in Arkansas."

"The weirdest part about the missing soldier's story is that they show up fifty years later in a remote area of the hills of Arkansas, near a small town called Caddo Gap. That's clear across the country from where they disappeared. Even more bizarre is that they had not aged a day the entire time they were gone. They looked the same as when they went to the Triangle in 1972.

I didn't tell you about another event but disappearing and coming back also happened to a nine-year-old boy named Truman Wallace, who was also found. We have kept his return a secret from the public for a few months now, trying to figure out what happened to him. While hiking in the forest with his parents, the boy disappeared in the Alaskan Triangle in 1997. Nothing was ever found of him, even after weeks of extensive searching.

We haven't told anyone, but he reappeared in the exact location where he disappeared a few months ago. Except now it is twenty-five years later. When found, he still looked as though he did when he disappeared at age nine. He, too, had not grown or aged. At first, he immediately wanted to be united with his family. However, his family had moved and no longer lived in the Alaskan area, so we had to locate their whereabouts.

After a few months of meetings with top military officials, Truman Wallace claims he lived with the Sungcut people in Alaska. He said he was raised in an underground cave in a state of euphoria located under Mt. Hayes. He also claimed he lived with people from the Nethers dimension. Truman told us that the people from both locations never age; they stay the same.

Once he and his family were together again, the parents only kept him for a few days. They called the military and had them take Truman back. They were angry with the army and the government for what they thought was some kind of conspiracy or a hoax. They returned him to us, saying he was not their son.

They believed the entire story told to them when they got him back was a lie or made-up fabrication staged by the government or military. When they turned him back to us, they said we needed to be honest about who this person was. They wanted to know why we did that to them after twenty-five years of trying to believe their son was dead and grieving the loss of their son." The father wanted to know, "Is this kid a clone, a new form of Artificial Intelligence, or something else? We just know he's not our son." Hiller said, "That's all they would say to us about him. We have kept him housed in one of our military facilities at Area 51, trying to figure out the mystery of his story and what to do with him."

The military wants to know how these people disappear and reappear years later without aging. We would also like to know how something like that is even possible. We want to see if it has something to do with time travel through a wormhole, interdimensional travel, or is it something they have been eating or drinking in their environment that has kept them young. We need to find the answer to these questions."

Zak said, "Yeah, those two stories are amazing. If I can find the answer to those questions, it could impact future travel. What is the first thing the military wants me to do, and what is their ultimate goal?"

Chuck replied, "We need to know how four military personnel got from Alaska to Arkansas and didn't age during those fifty years they were gone? We must also understand how Truman Wallace stayed the same age after twenty-five years.

I have to be honest with you, Zak. Everything we have talked about is undocumented and experimental grounds for us. If there are vortexes or interdimensional travel in these areas, we are unaware of them. I don't know if you can return if you get caught in that dimension or space in time.

Because we are unaware of how to enter or leave that vortex or dimension, you may be there for years and miss a life of being with your family if you get stuck there forever. It's all a huge mystery to us.

If you decide to take the mission, I will say the first thing you should do is interview these people and see if we can find out what has happened to them while they were missing. We want to know the answers."

Chapter 2 – The Sungcut people

Hiller spoke to Zak again on the phone and told him that Mt Hayes has a height of 14,000 feet and is located inside the triangle. It is the highest mountain in Alaska. There have been many U.F.O. sightings in that area, and the F.B.I. began investigating UFO sightings back in the 1940s. Some UFO enthusiasts believe the aliens have one of their largest bases on Earth under the mountain at Mt. Hayes. There may even be a vortex-like the ones at Sedona and Mt. Shasta. We don't know what is going on there, but recently we've gotten some unexplainable events that have taken place coming from the Triangle.

For years, we have received reports about a hidden race of "Little People" living and hiding in that part of the world. The local village elders from the area call them the Sungcut instead of the little people, and they claim they live deep in the ground under Mt. Hayes, inside the Alaskan Triangle.

The locals believe the Sungcut people are an alien race, but humans have misinterpreted them as nothing more than a race of little Earthly beings. Because we have not explored that area, it could be possible they are an alien race in the Mt. Hayes area and have been there for thousands of years.

It's believed they have protective powers and are said to possess control over natural forces and have the ability to extend a person's length of life through something they eat or drink or both." Zak said, "You mean something like the mysterious Fountain of Youth? Hiller replied, "Yes, just like that. They are also said to be strong and fast with supernatural strength and speed despite their small size, even though they are only about three and a half feet tall. "Zak, let me read you something here that gives a better picture of who these people are," Hiller said. Zak sat silently on the other end of the phone as captain Hiller continued.

"There is a story widely circulated in the Triangle villages that claim two experienced hunters were tracking a herd of Caribou for a while in the mountainous area when they finally caught up with the pack in a valley, grazing on tundra scrub. The two had left their snowmobiles and walked into the valley so as not to scare the Caribou with the noise. It was late in the afternoon, with the western sun illuminating the valley.

The men picked positions to take down their elected targets and bag their Caribou. One hunter used binoculars and checked out the herd from his vantage point. He spotted three hunters on the valley's far side despite the remote location. They had killed and were cleaning a large bull. The partner got the attention of the other hunter when he spotted them through the scope of his weapon. When he saw the hunters, he knew something was off. They were small, like little people, with large heads, short, muscular bodies, and wearing indigenous clothing, hand-made from hides. They were not carrying any visible guns.

When they spotted the hunters watching them, one of the little people pointed at them and threw the Caribou over his shoulders, and in an instant, they were gone. The two hunters went to the spot where they had seen the three little people and found only small splotches of blood around the area and tiny footprints, like those of children, scattered in a circle. There were no traces of tracks leading to or from that location.

Some villagers have stories about the little people that are haunting, and some are humorous. Some say little people have hassled them by pulling tricks on them, from the carefree to amusing. It has been told they tie villagers' hair in knots while sleeping and throw snowballs at them. Then they disappear right before their eyes, and much more.

One village in the Northwest, Shaktolik, is afraid of the Sungcut. They say they are protective, benevolent, spiteful, and vengeful. They believe anyone who sees one of the little people will go missing for at least a year or may never return. They claim the little people may account for a lot of the missing people because there are a lot of stories from locals that claim they have seen them, and some also claim to have been abducted by them. Some of the people abducted by the little people and returned years later say they never aged during their time away. The returnees claim to have lived in a paradise below the earth with their captors. They also claim that the little people could communicate with each other, but with outsiders through Telepathy."

When Hiller had finished the story, Zak said, "Most of that sounds like a lot of Folklore to me. Besides, what does it have to do with a mission the military wants me to undertake?" Hiller replied, "It could be easy to say that traveling through a rough and barren area may be the problem with missing people, but we believe our situation is more threatening and stranger than just missing people. All this may involve aliens, portals, vortexes, space travel, and extended life. With your experience with aliens, portals, and different dimensions, we think you can help us discover what is happening."

Chapter 3 - Defending Mankind

The Agency was created, innocently enough, in 1952, by President Truman's administration in response to the overwhelming public interest and fear in the emerging UFO phenomena. The thought behind the creation was that, should a legitimate alien presence visit the Earth, would peoples of the Earth be protected? Of course, the answer to that in the highest political echelons was a resounding no. There had never been a realistic defense to the possible threat other than the militaries of the Earth, notably the US Army and Air Force.

To better organize the group, high-ranking military officers and political and eminent scientists of the world were brought in and governed by twelve people. This clandestine organizational body became known as MJ-12 or the majestic twelve.

With the advent of sophisticated technologies that were developed in unison with the UFO phenomena, many overt agencies were tasked with the cleanup and coverup of a phenomenon of sorts itself, the recovery and back-engineering of crashed and captured alien crafts.

But the world's governments weren't prepared for their citizens to know of the alien existence or their origins and needed a covert agency to step into that role. Thus, "The Agency" was born and assumed the role.

Initially funded by The Department of Defense and the world bank, The Agency investigated and researched the UFO phenomena, the crafts that carried alien visitors, and ultimately the visitors themselves.

Then a strange thing happened in the mid-1960s. Along with the alien visitors that humans around the world were seeing, monsters, strange and horrifying, were also being sighted in various parts of the globe and were wreaking havoc here on Earth.

Once again, to address the growing problem, the Majestic Twelve (12) created a combat force within the agency to confront the growing concern. Consisting of soldiers from various military forces from around the world, mainly the United States, they recruited heavily from the Navy Seals, the Marine Corp, and the Army Rangers. Currently headed by Colonial Matthew Simmons of the US Army Rangers and overseen by General Wendel Conners and the US Department of Homeland Security. It was slowly becoming a subset of the newly formed US Space Force.

Zak Thomas had come aboard three years earlier, joining the agency after two tours of duty in Afghanistan and Iraq with the US Army Ranger's unique details unit. He had mustered out of service as a staff Sargent and then went to work for the Washington State Forest Service. After a severe encounter with monsters created and sent to Earth by Alien visitors and his unique training and skills developed while in the Rangers. The Agency approached and recruited him as a combat soldier and hunter for their organization, a Gunnery Sargent with the US Army Rangers, and a member of The Agency.

Working closely with Colonel Simmons and his staff along with the colonel's aide, Captain Chuck Hiller, Zak felt they made a good team and trusted the duty assignments given to him, even with the occasional ribbing they gave him by calling him, "The Monster Hunter," a moniker he had earned in Afghanistan while hunting and eventually killing a crazed Afghani serial killer for the military.

Having been sent on several international assignments with varied success, he was now asked to step into an area of extreme puzzlement and awe for Mankind, the question of everlasting life.

After talking to Julie, Zak talked to Chuck on the phone again and said, "Julie and I are ok with me accepting this next assignment, but there is something we both want the military to do for us." Chuck said, "Shoot, and I'll see what I can do." Zak told him that he and Julie wanted a room installed in their spare bedroom like a bank vault. It had to be a ten-foot square room made of thick eight-inch metal. They felt if they were attacked at home by one of Zak's enemies, like what happened to Julie the last time, they had to have protection.

The alien came to Julie in the form of a shadow person in the night, but she was able to get away from his attack. They didn't want to take any chances in case something like that happened again. They had to have a safe place they could take refuge not only for themselves but for Christopher. It had to be a room that nobody could penetrate with a handheld weapon. It also had to have a phone system that once the door was shut and locked, there was a direct phone call to Hiller, and Simmons dialed automatically. Hiller said, "I'll put the order in for it immediately." Zak said, "Thank you, Chuck, that will make me feel better about my wife and son's safety while I'm on my mission."

Two weeks later, the military showed up at Zak and Julie's house with the metal building padded inside. It was on a flatbed truck with a large crane attached so they could open up the roof and drop the vault room inside. Once it was installed in the room, they patched up the hole in the top, so you couldn't tell they had ever placed the metal room inside. They made sure there were no leaks in the ceiling. Inside the door were two large flashlights and extra batteries attached to the wall. On the other side were three oxygen tanks with masks firmly attached by straps.

They spent time and showed Julie how to close the door and lock it and how the phones worked. Zak got a call from Julie to let him know it had been installed and was working well. Zak called Hiller and thanked him for getting the room done and making Julie feel safe.

While on the phone, Zak said, "I would like to talk to the nine-year-old boy and the four soldiers as soon as possible. Chuck replied, "I will arrange for you to meet nine-year-old Truman Wallace and the four soldiers when ready. Just let me know."

Chapter 4 – The Passage

A small craft moved through space. Its single occupant
was preoccupied with focus on utilizing the devices the
craft employed to create stealth as it moved in position to
enter the Earth's stratosphere. Interestingly, the vehicle
resembled the Lockheed F-117 Nighthawk, also known as
the stealth fighter. The pilot hoped this similarity would
familiarize or confuse the planet's aircraft controllers in his
dissent to Earth. This craft was much more powerful than
the F-117 and far more advanced in speed and agility.
Though the aircraft share similar technology, they could
reduce radar and radio frequency, creating a stealth effect
and a sense of cloaking, but they were vastly different.

As the craft entered into Earth's atmosphere, the ship's
control panel showed a grid for the southeastern state of
Florida and specifically the isolated area of the Everglades.

Dan Mathers and his ten-year-old son, Donnie, were
working on the far eastern area of Florida City that
bordered the Florida Everglades. They had come to the site
to collect swamp wood Dan used to shape his wooden
sculptured creations, which he sold throughout the Eastern
coastal Florida communities.

"Daddy, I'm going to go a little closer into the swamp,"
Donnie said to his father. "Ok, but stay away from the
water until I get there. I want to check it for gators," Dan
responded.

The day was bright, and Donnie could see many pieces of
the Florida pinewood scattered on the edge of the deep
swamp. The swamp spread before him and ran as far as his

eye could see. A giant Heron flew lazily overhead and landed on a jutting branch of a tall dead pine.

In the distance, Donnie saw an object that looked like a round disc that seemed to float to the ground as it landed in the swamp. It sank into the water so it couldn't be seen. He didn't think much about what it could have been because he was preoccupied. Several minutes later, he saw what he thought might be another animal making its way through the swamp. But as it came closer, he saw it walking upright like a man. Suddenly Donnie was overcome with fear, for he had heard the stories of the half-human creature, the swamp ape, the entire time he was growing up in Florida. This figure didn't resemble so much the mythical being he'd heard about but looked more like a human person. It walked through the low-water areas upright and purposeful while it was intense, not leisurely, on the land.

Seeing it come closer, Donnie turned and ran back to the area his father stood sorting the wood they had collected. "Daddy, daddy!" He yelled as he neared his father. "There's something out walking in the swamp. I think it might be a swamp ape or a person," he gasped as he halted to a stop. He was looking at his father in profound earnest. Knowing his son was honest and not given to be a prankster, Dan looked up in the direction of the swamp and said, "Let's go," as they both headed down the path Donnie had just taken.

Arriving at the swamp water's edge, Dan peered left and right, hoping to glance at the figure before it had gone. "Where was it, son?" Dan said while scanning left and right and shielding his eyes with his right hand to block the sun's glare. "Right through there," Donnie said as he pointed ahead at approximately two o'clock. Dan continued to scan but couldn't see anything. "It must've gone. Damn, do you think it might've been the ape?" Dan said as he looked over at his son. "I don't know," Donnie shrugged. "Well, let's get back. It's time to head home anyway. Dan looked around to take a last look before they left.

Making their way through the grasses on an improvised trail, Dan asked, "What do you want for dinner? I'll call ahead and ask your mom?" Mom said she is making fried chicken with mashed potatoes." Donnie said, smiling broadly, "Yum." Dan said, smiling himself.

And then, looking up from the path, he could see their wood pile, but his Jeep Cherokee was nowhere in sight in the distance. "What the hell?" Dan said as he ran to the roadway. But his car was gone. "Son of a b.." Dan yelled but caught himself as he looked over at Donnie. Then taking his cell phone from his pocket, he called 911 and said, "Yes, I would like to report my car was just stolen by someone."

The driver of the stolen Jeep Cherokee sat stone-faced as the vehicle traveled along the dark two-lane highway. He glanced to his right as he passed a posted road sign showing Florida City 10 miles ahead, and a slight smile formed on his mouth. But no other emotion escaped him. No remorse for being far from home. No thoughts of personal pleasures. Only his singular focus for his mission was to find La Fuente de Juventud, the natural substance indigenous to Earth that, when consumed, shows signs of therapeutic properties and even rumors of longevity. No matter the cost or risk, he would have that substance, and no resident of this world dare stop him.

His research found that many explorers of this planet had sought the substance. Several had come close and recounted stories of personal encounters, but none so illustrious, adventuresome, and convincing as Hermando de Soto. This conquistador explorer wrote about many exploits, particularly in the Arkansas mountainous area that held this treasure which grew to be known as the legendary Fountain of Youth.

Siratchik became so obsessed and transfixed with de Soto's exploits; being an explorer himself, he modified the name and took to calling himself DeSoto after the famous explorer. Now the name of DeSoto became his own.

During his research, he also found that Nether travelers to Earth had collected this substance, developed it into medicines, and combined it with elements of compounds from their world. They have used it extensively for themselves and their people. But they always tended to be tight-lipped about the truth or information regarding the life extension substance.

One specific thing is that the Netters lived inordinately long healthy lives. DeSoto wanted that knowledge and ability for himself. He knew he couldn't get the information from his fellow Nethers, but his obsession with acquiring the information's secrets drove him forward. He couldn't stop himself because he knew having the formula from the substance would make him rich and give him immense power.

Not getting the information from his people made him realize that he had to travel to Earth and get what he wanted from the Earthlings.

Chapter 5 – DeSoto visits Austin's Home

Pulling into Florida City, DeSoto pulled off the highway onto a residential side street and made his way into the center portion of town that contained the city's older section.

The night was cut by the illumination of the street's lights, but this house had a fairly dark carport that would work for now. He pulled the Jeep into the empty area in the carport next to an old Ford Ranger truck. He ejected the index finger size device he had inserted into the critical mechanism that started the vehicle, and the car shut down immediately. Then stepping out into the darkness, he glanced around and up and down the street and saw no sign of life or movement.

Making his way around the side of the house, he opened the feeble lock on the wooden gate, skirted through along the six-foot fence, then moved to the side of the house that wrapped around the patio. Stepping onto the deck, he could see an aged slider door, long neglected and grimy dirty, where the handle and lock set. Pulling on the handle, DeSoto discovered it to be unlocked and able to be opened but stopped with a dull thud.

A wooden broomstick, minus the whisk, caught the door an inch open. The slight smile again formed on DeSoto's mouth, and he reached into his bag and, kneeling, created a ten-inch metal object into a horseshoe, and putting it near the wooden stick, he quietly and quickly flipped it out of the runner.

Just as quietly, he slipped through the door but cut his finger on a small metal shard as he entered. He pulled a small tube from his pocket containing a green salve-looking substance. He put a small amount on his right forefinger and rubbed it on the cut. It immediately stopped bleeding and started healing instantly.

He made his way into the house, where he found a darkened corner of the living room which sat a recliner, and he turned and sat in it to observe his surroundings. At 2:00 AM, Austin's current main squeeze, Tamara Gibbens, ambled downstairs and made her way to the kitchen. Opening the refrigerator, she took out an imported beer and a generous slice of Chocolate cake on a paper plate with the partial name of Tamara written in cursive across it. Opening the beer and grabbing a fork, she made her way to the living room couch, the flimsy robe freely flowing, exposing nothing worn underneath. Setting the items on the oak coffee table to one side, she pulled a wooden cigar box towards her, holding several bagged ounces of marijuana Austin sold at the In and Out Club to supplement his income. Removing one of the bags from the box, Tamara opened it and, fumbling for rolling papers inside, began to roll a joint.

She heard a slight noise and looked up, "Who the fuck are you?" She asked, staring at Desoto sitting in the recliner in the corner of the room. Desoto stood and aimed his hand-held Ion Laser pistol at Tamara's neck center and fired, which cut a perfect one-inch hole clean through her neck and cauterized the wound so precisely that it left the area bloodless. It also left Tamara trying to breathe and dying in shock and suffocation.

Desoto glancing up toward the stairway, grabbed his bag and, with a pistol in hand, made his way to Austin's bedroom. DeSoto felt the chilly morning temperature as he ascended the stairs, and a central heating system kicked on, but no other sound emanated from the house.

Approaching an open doorway that led to a bedroom, DeSoto quietly peered inside the darkened room, which lay a man on a bed covered by a blanket. DeSoto walked around the bed with the Ion pistol in hand and leveled it at the sleeping figure, and then putting his foot on the bed next to the sleeper, pressed the bed up and down vigorously, waking the man, who quickly sat up and yelled, "What the hell." Staring straight ahead, he could see no one and then turned to face DeSoto, who stood looking down at Burrows while still pointing the pistol at him.

The two stared at each other for a moment, then DeSoto asked, "Are you Austin Burrows, the guide?" Austin, taken back by the confrontation, stammered, "I'm Austin. What's going on? Where's Tamara?" DeSoto sat on the side of the bed and motioned for Austin to sit back against the wall. "You are a guide that took many trips through Florida and boasted that you know where to find the Fountain of Youth?" Desoto asked while studying Austin's face. "Fountain of Youth? What the fuck?" "Look, pal, that's shit I said for my customers back then. It was just marketing; I don't even do that shit anymore! I'm a bartender now. What are you looking for, man?" Austin pleaded. "So, you do not know the Fountain or the Algae associated with the substance?" Desoto asked. "No, man, I don't know a fucking thing about any of that kind of shit. Now get out of my house." Austin commanded, feeling a tad braver. Desoto continued to study Austin's face, particularly his eyes.

Seeing this human was of no benefit to him, he said, "Alright," and then he shot Austin through the forehead with the Ion ray pistol. It did the same thing it had done with Tamara, cut a perfectly cauterized hole that killed Austin instantly, much like getting hit in the head with a ball pin sledgehammer. Austin fell backward with his eyes staring wide open. DeSoto went over to him and used his right forefinger to close Austin's eyes. He said, "You should have given me what I wanted."

Desoto then went down the stairs and retraced his steps out of the back slider door to return to the front. He then opened the door to Tamara's old Ford Ranger pickup. He inserted his device, which instantly started the vehicle, and began to drive back to his craft for his next destination, Miami, Florida.

Chapter 6 – Miami Blues

Charlio and DJ sat at a small table overlooking the bank along the south Beach Miami waterfront. The sun glared down on the men but was not unpleasant, and the tiny umbrella above the table cast a slight shadow to break the glare. Two-blade skaters skimmed by with their polyester suits tight against their skin.

Charlio, feeling slightly drunk, took another drink of his Mai Tai, pushing the small cocktail umbrella aside that held a generous chunk of pineapple. Then glancing over at DJ, he asked, "Dude, what does DJ stand for?" DJ, facing the ocean, with his head slightly tilted back and his eyes closed, catching the sun's rays, replied, "I'm a DJ," and remained silent.

"Bullshit," Charlio fired back. "I've known you for three years, and I haven't seen you disc jockey once," Charlio added. DJ turned his head to the right and opened his eyes, "Back in my younger days, late ninety's, MP-3 stuff. The initials stand for Douglas Johnston," DJ finally said. "Damn, dude, that's Hollywood shit," Charlio said in his sharpest Cuban accent. "I knew you were from

Connecticut or some such place, but this," Charlio chuckled as he continued to talk.

"With a name like that, you could've even been a writer or mayor, but here you are, you ain't shit, just a common desperado." Charlio then started to laugh aloud as DJ looked over at him.

Then DJ's cell phone rang his familiar Eighties pop song ringtone. DJ put his hand up with his index finger extended to motion Charlio to freeze, which Charlio instantly did and strained to hear any of the callers' words. "Uh-huh, got it," DJ said into the phone, then pressed END as he looked over at Charlio and said, "Herb is going to send over information on where to meet him in a few minutes. We gotta roll." They stood up and went down the promenade to DJ's car.

Herb Kershaw moved his hand over the iPad, which lit brightly. The apps lined the page and stared back in excited anticipation, "pick me," they implied. Herb pressed the icon, which brought up the local map of retail gun shops, scaled down to Noble Sporting Goods, and transferred the address to his associate's email address.

Then calling his partner, he asked, "Did you get the info I just sent?" His associate grunted back his positive response. "You and Charlio, meet me there in one hour." He then killed the call and stepped out of his hotel room.

As he took his next step from his left, an arm swung hard against his throat, hitting him and forcing him back into the room, flaying him backward as he put his hands up to his throat area. DeSoto stepped into the room and hurriedly shut the front door behind him. Herb, who lay against the bed, grabbed the 9 mm Glock pistol in his belt holster, but

DeSoto quickly kicked the gun from Herb's weak grip, and the weapon flew to one side of the room.

DeSoto knelt and, facing Herb, who was now in a fair amount of visible pain, began to rub his wrist. "You sell guns and explosives!" DeSoto quietly said as he stared at Herb. Herb, looking into this stranger's face, was uneasy. The face was regular but off, strange, especially the eyes. They were like sharks' eyes, dark and menacing. "And I'm not talking about legal guns either," DeSoto added. "I don't know." Herb started to say, but DeSoto promptly stopped him and said a little louder, "I need them now." Herb, no longer feeling the desire to put up a fight further, simply said, "Ok, you could've just asked, but his small show of bravado could not mask his fear of this stranger. "They're not cheap, but I have what you're asking for in a small warehouse on the north end of town," Herb said.

The two looked at each other for a moment, then DeSoto said, "Let's go." "Alright, alright," Herb shouted as he fumbled for his footing. "Wait, hold up," Herb suddenly said, "I've got to call someone, a business associate," he said with an air of urgency. "Just to let him know, I won't be meeting him." DeSoto walked over to Herbs Glock, picked it up, walked back over to Herb, and pressed it against Herb's temple. DeSoto then said, "Make it fast and make it simple. I speak your language." Herb, looking a little puzzled, replied he would.

Herb's call to DJ was received coolly and with no argument. Herb told DJ that he and Charlio to head to their homes or wherever they wanted, but he couldn't meet them tonight. Plans changed; he'd talk with them tomorrow. DJ, being of a suspicious mind, just knew something was up and refused to let it go. "I know that bastard is going to do something without us, DJ thought. Probably going to run by the warehouse to pick up merch to sell. I know that's what he's doing." His thoughts ran on as he became more agitated.

Turning to Charlio, he said, "Herb canceled tonight's meet. I'm tired, gonna head home," he said after a pause. "Want me to drop you off somewhere?" He asked Charlio. Charlio looked disappointed but said, "No man, I'm going to stick around the promenade, make a night of it, get some poon," and flashed a big smile as he exited the car. DJ flashed a hand wave as he pulled out into the street. But DJ had no intention of heading home and gunned his engine as he threaded into traffic, heading for the north side of Miami.

When DJ pulled up to the warehouse on the north end, he saw Herb's car parked on the side street and knew his suspicions were confirmed. "I knew it, that son of a bitch," he mumbled angrily.

Driving a block further, he pulled to the curb and shut off the engine. Pulling out the older model Bulldog 44 pistol he kept under his seat, he checked to ensure it was fully loaded and stuck it in his right blazer pocket. He then casually walked back to the warehouse in the shadows.

Herb only turned on the barest of light in the warehouse, not wanting to draw attention to his activities. After all, he was the renter of the property, but no use bringing more attention than needed.

"What's your name, buddy?" Herb asked, seeking to build a friendly rapport. "You can call me DeSoto," DeSoto answered back. Now Herb thought he had connected the dots, "DeSoto?" Latin. That's why he said he spoke our language. Herb thought, "What are you, Columbian?"

"Makes sense. You have a project you're working on; I could help you with that," Herb said, his criminal mind already looking for a way to make fast money. "You will, Herb," DeSoto replied. "Here is a list of what I want. Fill it with what you have. If you slight me, I'll be unforgiving," DeSoto added.

"Yeah, I've heard that about you Colombians," Herb shot back, and scanning the list, he said, "Hey, this merchandise is not going to be cheap. Let me see your green." DeSoto pulled out a large wad of American currency from his bag, mainly one-hundred-dollar bills folded over and held by a silver clip, and showed it to Herb. That'll do it," Herb said with a broad grin and walked to the back of the warehouse, looking at the list and pulling out the items on the shelves.

To DJ's disappointment, Herb had never allowed him to have a key to the warehouse but always assured him he was an equal partner in their enterprise. It caused many arguments. DJ was undeterred and didn't sweat it. His first ten years of criminal activity involved B and E's, and he was good at what he did. DJ had to leave Connecticut, too much breaking and entering. He tried the warehouse door handle, and as expected, it was locked, but he knelt and went to work on it and had it open in a matter of seconds. Herb had disabled the alarm inside the building, so it was easily breached, and DJ slid inside.

As DJ worked his way around the boxes and rows of shelves, Herb had just completed filling DeSoto's order and carried a box containing the items over to where DeSoto Stood. "Alright, amigo, you're looking right at, and let's round this out, ten grand even. That was about the amount you had in that roll. When Herb looked down at DeSoto's hand holding the cash, he saw a weapon he had never seen before in DeSoto's other hand. "What the hell is that weapon?" he asked, admiring the pistol while sitting the box down. He asked, "Can I see it?" DeSoto looked at his Ion ray pistol and said, "I doubt if you would know how to work it," then pointing it upward, he fired a concentrated beam of pure energy that tore through Herb's upper torso, which created a one-inch cauterized hole clean through Herb's heart. Herb fell to one side, dying instantly, having half of his heart severed in the blast.

DJ, having witnessed the scene and already highly agitated by what he thought was a double-cross by Herb, quickly pulled out his Bulldog 44 and yelled, "Freeze, you motherfucker." DeSoto, not surprised by this intrusion, knowing that Herb had associates, faded sideways and went into shadow effect. Although still able to be seen as a shadow in the dim light, it gave him just enough time to flank DJ, who stood momentarily confused by the stranger. Still, DeSoto was quicker, and his Ion pistols blast caught DJ in the left side of his head, punching a perfect bloodless hole in his brain.

DeSoto walked over to DJ's body, picked up the 44 and Herb's empty Glock in his waist belt, and tossed them in the items Herb had accumulated for him. He then picked up the box and pistol in hand and stepped out of the warehouse to Herb's car to head back to his ship, buried several feet under the muddy water of the Everglade swamp.

In his research, he found out about the four soldiers found in the Ozark Mountains that hadn't aged during the entire fifty years they were gone. He knew they had to be connected to the Fountain of Youth and the substance he was searching to find.

Chapter 7 – Zak follows a lead to Florid

The next day Zak got a call from his commanding officer and friend, Colonel Simmons. When he came on the phone, the Colonel said, "I know Hiller talked to you about the Little People and that mission, but I wanted to talk to you about something that popped up this morning. We must put the little people on hold until we figure out this new incident. We have several killings in the Everglades of Florida, and the deaths appear to be from an advanced weapon. Much like the advanced weapons, certain specialized military soldiers are now using. The wounds show an advanced death pattern like the cauterized wounds seen on the mutilated cattle reports. We need your help in solving this matter. The wounds could also be from an alien weapon used."

Zak was a little confused about why they wanted him to investigate if the wounds were done by an extra-terrestrial or by a human using alien technology. He felt they could get any soldier to research those kinds of murders.

Sensing Zak's apprehension, the Colonel said, "Look, Zak, there is a lot more to the cattle mutilations that not even top military members know. The information I will give you must be just between us." Zak laughed and said, "That's never a problem with me, Colonel. Nobody would believe me anyway." The Colonel continued, "From 1954 to 1992, the United States did atomic bomb testing. To be exact, 215 exploded above ground and 815 below ground in places like Nevada, Alaska, Mississippi, Colorado, and New Mexico. Not only did the damn bombs kill numerous soldiers and civilians in America, but they also caused severe nuclear fallout. The atomic fallout agents are known to cause cell changes in humans and cause cancer. Nuclear agents have been discovered in the milk supply of cattle, and kids have been the most vulnerable because they drink so much of the milk in America. The livestock eats contaminated plants or drinks infected water and milk, and the people eat the meat.

The damn cattle mutilations thing is a covert operation done by black ops people and is not shared with the military or anyone. All we know is they go out with black helicopters in remote areas, pick up cattle, and then carry them to a different location where they drain their blood and cut out their tongues and other vital parts like their ears, utters, etc. They then drop them back where they were initially taken. They continually test and monitor how many parts per million of the isotopes are still in the cattle parts. So far, they have implied and fooled the public into thinking that aliens may have something to do with these mutilations.

We've never seen wounds on people like the ones on the bodies from Florida before, cattle, but not people. We need to determine if a rogue alien serial killer was responsible for these deaths and is on the loose. If it's a related black ops agent, we need to know that as well. With your experience and past success with tracking and recon, this should be right up your alley. We have four bodies you can examine that are sitting in our morgue down in Florida. Three men and a woman. The sooner you could take a look at them, the better."

Zak replied, "Ok, Colonial, I will get on this case tomorrow. I will let Julie know I'm taking the mission and fill her in as well. Can you have Hiller line up my transportation to the location of the bodies?" "Yes, it will be done, and he will be in touch with you tomorrow morning. He turned to Hiller and said, "Sargent Thomas will be ready in the morning, so make sure he has everything he needs. We need to get to the bottom of this to ensure it doesn't become something out of hand." Hiller agreed and said, "I will take care of everything, Sir." The Colonial told Zak good luck before he hung up the phone.

The following day at 0600, he was picked up by a black helicopter and transported to the nearest military base so he could fly to an Air Force Base in Florida. The local authorities had turned the four bodies over to the military personnel to be autopsied. They were being held at the Air Force Base near the Everglades.

When Zak arrived, he was led to a metal frame building where a physician met him and Hiller at the entry to the building. Zak saw three males and one woman lying on four metal slabs with white sheets pulled loosely over their bodies.

Zak walked over to the first body, and as he lifted the sheet to look at the body, the physician said, "These people were shot and killed by some laser or energy-directed weapon. Those types of weapons have not been disbursed to our regular soldiers yet. Zak saw that they were perfectly cut and cauterized with precision. He was fully aware of these types of wounds because he had seen them before when he fought with the aliens in the past. He had even used one of the weapons during his last mission.

He went over to the body of Austin Burrows and Tamara Gibbens. After a pause, he leaned over Austin's upper torso and asked, "Did you notice this small tint of a green substance near his eyes? The physician bent down closer and looked at the spot Zak had pointed out. He said, "Yes, we got as much of it as possible and sent it off to be analyzed. We're waiting for the results to see what it may be."

Zak said, "You are correct, doctor. Some type of advanced weapon did these wounds." He turned and whispered to Hiller, "I have to find out if the weapon was one of ours or if it was alien in origin. Based on the green substance I'm seeing on the victim's body, I believe it to be alien because the Nether showed me a substance that resembled that color. They claimed it had healing powers. What was it doing on the victim? It looks like the killer may have inadvertently got it on Austin's eyes after he killed him."

He asked, "Do you have the names and addresses of these four victims?" The physician said, "Yes, we have all of them for you in these folders, and he handed them to Hiller." Zak took the folders from Captain Hiller and said, "We need to go out in the field and investigate why these individuals would be a target of an alien attack."

After spending several days digging around, he discovered the story of Donnie and his dad. Dan had been telling people in that area about a skunk ape stealing their car. As crazy as it sounded, Zak made an appointment with Dan and his son so he could find out for himself about what had happened to them.

Talking to them for a few hours, Zak had them take him to the area where Donnie had seen the creature. He told Zak, "I saw some craft come down out of the sky and go into the water, but it sank fast." He pointed to the area where he had seen it last. He said, "It wasn't long after that when I saw the Skunk Ape walking toward the shore. It scared me so much I ran yelling to my dad about the creature." He told Zak it looked more like a person than any type of Bigfoot or Skunk Ape.

When Zak got back to Base, he was shown a room for the night, and standing next to the small desk, he called

Colonial Simmons and told him he believed an alien was responsible for the deaths of the four individuals in Florida. Still, he couldn't establish the motivation or connection behind the attacks. He told the Colonial he would stick around for a few days and find out if he could dig up something.

Chapter 8 - Hop, Skip, and a Jumper

Zak always felt himself to be pretty patient, and God knows how many stakeouts he had covered in his tracking exploits of various villains he had hunted. This incident was one time he couldn't and wouldn't sit still and wait for the next victim to surface. And besides, time was of the essence. But where to start? Where to pick up a lead?

He knew he had to jump on this before the trail went cold, and he figured the best direction would be at the crime site itself. And that landed him in Florida City at one of the victims, Austin Burrow's house.

The house was located in an older city section and had moved into the third phase of development, decline. It was given to Austin by his mother at her death. She had inherited it from her mother and father, who had moved into the new home in early 1931. It received a little less love through the generations than the previous tenant. When Austin took occupancy, it screamed for the fourth phase: Renewal.

Zak stepped up the steps to the massive oak front door and briskly knocked on the door, seeing no doorbell. After what seemed like an overly long delay, and just as Zak was again going to knock, the door flung wide open. A behemoth stood wearing a tight black tank top, faded jeans tucked in black biker boots, and slicked black hair raked back and plastered down by days of unwashed wear.

As he stood there and glared at Zak, he finally blared, "Yes?" Zak, momentarily taken back, almost went into a defensive position but immediately realized that was both foolish and futile. "I'm Zak Thomas with Homeland Security and looking for." "She already gave the Godamn police her statement," the behemoth yelled, cutting off Zak's intro. "Let em in, Paul," a voice behind the man commanded.

Paul stepped aside, and Zak could see a middle-aged, once attractive woman reclined on the couch. With her hand holding a cigarette and the other a TV remote, she motioned to Zak to sit in Austin's recliner as she said, "I'm Austin's sister, Betty. What can I do for you, Mr. Thomas?"

Zak sat on the old recliner, looked around the room, then focused on Betty and asked, "Do you mind if I ask you a few questions, Betty?" The woman shifted her position, leaned over, and put her cigarette in the ashtray on the coffee table. "I get it. You don't share information, different departments, and that kind of shit, shoot," she replied.

"Do you live in the house, Betty?" Zak asked as he settled back. "I do now. I took possession after Austin died. I used to have an apartment a few blocks from here." Betty quickly answered back. "I had come by to check on my brother, and that's when I found the bodies a few days ago, she added. (In truth, she had come by to pick up her weekly ounce of weed). "Did you see or notice anything unusual?" Zak asked.

"Aside from a couple of dead bodies?" Betty asked, then added, "But I wasn't in the house long. I contacted the police and hung around outside. Felt creepy being in with the dead." Zak continued to look at her and then looked up at the stairwell, which the report stated led up to the bedroom where Austin's body was found. "Did Austin have any friends I could talk with that might have more information for me?" Zak asked. "Austin had a ton of acquaintances, but friends, not so much," she continued as she leaned over and lit another cigarette. Then she added, reaching up and removing a speck of tobacco from her tongue tip. "He was closest to his bartender buddy at the In and Out Club, Tommy Tone. He'll most likely be the one that would know if Austin had enemies.

Zak thanked her and wrote down his cell number in case she heard anything else, and as he stood to leave, Betty added, "And Mr. Thomas, be careful. The club can be a little dangerous." Zak could see she had a slight smile as she said that, and he slightly smiled as he nodded and stood to leave. Then making sure he didn't piss off Paul, he walked to the door and down the steps as he exited and walked toward his rental car, determined to find the In and Out Club.

The In and Out club was just as Zak had envisioned, "A dive by any other name is still a dive." He had seen them from Subic Bay in the Philippines to Washington DC. They were all the same. To service and promote extreme vice. But this proprietorship had the advantage of being in the historical part of Florida City, giving it an air of character. Zak inwardly chuckled at this oxymoron.

Walking into the club though, he was surprisingly corrected. It did exude a confident air. It was the bar which was a wraparound and made of an old-weathered wood. Standing on one side of the bar flanked by his female counterpart stood a tall ultra-thin Rock and Roll type adorned with bracelets of various designs and piercings in multiple places. His short jet-black hair flipped back in a steep flourish. Zak knew this had to be Tommy Tone.

Zak walked to the bar and sat on a stool in front of Tommy, next to two young women on bar stools to his right. "What can I get for you?" Tommy asked as he slapped down a bar napkin. "Beer," Zak replied and asked, "Are you, Tommy?" "Yes, who's asking," Tommy shot back as he rubbed a much-used rag on the counter before him. "I'm Zak. I'm an investigator looking into Austin Burrow's death," Zak said as Tommy rubbed and listened. "Austin's sister said you two were friends?" Zak continued.

"More like work associates, Austin didn't have any close friends, but he knew everybody. He could be a real prick sometimes, like most people, but he and I got along pretty well," Tommy answered. "Did he have any enemies?" Zak asked. Tommy stopped and looked up to the ceiling, "Enemies?" "Well, a few years ago, when Austin was doing his touring scam, he took a few parties around the Everglades looking for the famous Fountain of Youth," Tommy said with a chuckle as he continued. "Of course, they never found anything, but he got bank for that, and he even did a couple of tours in Arkansas on the old DeSoto trail, really made out on those tours as well, and I'm sure he pissed those people off as well." "What town in Arkansas did Austin do the tours? Zak asked. "Funny ass name," Tommy laughed, "It's called Caddo Gap," Zak repeated the town's name back to himself, "Caddo Gap." "Any names in that town he dealt with," Zak asked. "No," Tommy said, pouring a beer on tap for Zak and setting it on the bar." "Oh, and there was this one asshole Austin occasionally did business with in Miami that had his goons beat him last year so badly he had to be hospitalized. He's someone you should look into," Tommy added.

"Do you remember his name?" Zak asked. "Wouldn't forget it," Tommy said, "His name is Herb Fucking Kershaw," Tommy said, as he strolled down the bar to another patron. A lightning bolt shot through Zak as though a light lit brightly in his brain. "I'll be damn, my first lead," Zak thought.

Zak now felt he had a legitimate lead and direction he could pursue and slapped a twenty-dollar bill on the table by the beer Tommy had given him. As he stood to leave, seated to his right were two Latin men where once the two girls sat. They were also eyeing Zak intensely, like they had bad intentions.

"What do you want with Austin, man?" the first seated man asked with a heavy Spanish accent. Zak looked at the men, smiled, and then walked to the club's exit. The men stood from the stools and looked slightly bewildered, then insulted. The first man mumbled something in Spanish, then they both followed behind Zak as he exited and walked toward his rental parked at the club's side.

Once outside, one of the men yelled to Zak, "Hey Puta, I'm speaking to you, don't turn your back on me, dude." Zak stopped and did an about-face. "What's on your mind?" Zak asked. "Like I said, what do you want with Austin?" the man shot back. "What you asked is none of your business," Zak countered. "Wrong motherfucker, Austin was a business associate of mine. It's all my business." The man shot back. Zak asked, "Do you know how he died?" "For all I know, it was your ass that killed him," the man said, advancing closer to Zak. At this point, the second man started rapidly walking toward Zak, fully displaying his angry intent.

As the man entered Zak's personal space, Zak did a roundhouse kick that landed squarely against the man's head and knocked him to the gravel. The first man, already advancing and close to Zak, pulled a holstered Glock pistol from his belt. But Zak's Taekwondo had kicked in, and he was in a fast run and jumped fully onto the man and wrestled him down, throwing the pistol aside. The man, startled by this sudden attack, fought to gain footing and struggled to his feet. Zak was already on his feet and standing close to the highly agitated man.

"I'm going to fuck you up bad, dude," the man yelled as he jumped to his feet and entered a right-handed boxing position. Zak changed from his ready stance to a left-handed boxing stance and waited for the man to lunge. He did with his right hand that Zak blocked with his left forearm and followed through with a right hook that connected and knocked the man backward, who stumbled to his knees. Once again, the man struggled to his feet and tried to regain his boxing stance but was shaken and unsteady on his feet. "Had enough?" Zak asked. "Eat Shit," the man said, then glanced over at his pistol lying on the gravel and took a weak run to get it in his hand.

At that moment, two men exited the club and quickly walked toward Zak and the Spanish man. Seeing the gun near the man to the right, they circled and headed back toward the club entrance. Zak stepped on the pistol and the man's hand as the man yelled Spanish obscenities.

Zak then motioned the man up, and as the man stood, Zak executed a high dropkick and caught the man under the chin, who once again dropped to the ground, this time not getting up, knocked senselessly. Zak then turned toward his vehicle, picked up the Glock, disassembled it in seconds, and threw it to the side.

Then stepping into the car, he programmed the GPS for Miami and prepared to drive on, feeling satisfied in this new direction. He briefly called the doctor and asked him if he had the results of the substance found in Austin's eyes. The doctor told Zak they got back their results but could not identify them because they contained a combination of different compounds. Zak asked him if it was some powder or a salve. He said it was like a salve. Zak thanked him, hung up the phone, and leaned back in his seat. He whispered to himself, "That stuff has to be alien and most likely the substance similar to what the Nethers showed me they possessed. But what was it doing to one of those victims?" Was the killer a Nether or someone that had stolen a portion of the secret from them?"

Chapter 9 – Searching for the Formula

The world of the Nether rotated on its axis. Its atmosphere glistened, clouded, brilliant in the blue-green hues given off by its double moons. The bejeweled streets reflecting the one sun shimmered. All was well.

Nether had always been held in high esteem by the myriad of worlds surrounding the known universe. The citizen's moral and character attitudes stood as beacons for the multitudes throughout the universe. The people of the Nether had existed for thousands of years and had advanced technologies developed for centuries. One of the things that stood out was their mode of travel. Although able to travel long distances with their highly developed ships, they preferred interdimensional travel, being quicker and more practical.

A restriction had long been imposed on the citizens that any interdimensional travel would first have to be approved by the state. But as with many worlds, there is good and evil, and the criminal element broke the rules and traveled at will.

When DeSoto summoned his comrades for a mission to Earth, the two Nethers who had worked with DeSoto in the past knew that he was capable and would not ask for their assistance unless he had something profitable for all of them. But DeSoto held his cards close to his sleeve and only gave them the barest of facts. Nonetheless, they followed his instructions and departed in their long-held inter-dimensional craft for Earth to the area of Florida City.

DeSoto had instructed the two of them to go to a local club called the In-N-Out Club, and once there, they would find known associates of Austin Burrows, which DeSoto said was someone of interest to him. The information they were to secure from the club was who Austin Burrow's known associates were and to interrogate them for additional information.

As the two Nethers sat at the long wooden bar, a man walked up and sat on the stool to the right and started to engage in conversation with the bartender. Just as quickly, two more men sat down at the two stools to the man's right, and the Nethers could hear the conversation between the stranger and the bartender. Then quickly, the stranger stood up and started to exit the club, and the two men to his right tried to engage him in conversation, but he wouldn't have any of it.

As he walked towards the exit and went outside, the two men to his right followed him. After a short period, the two

Nethers exited the club, but when they walked outside, they could see an altercation between the men, and one of the men was looking to the ground to retrieve his weapon. The Nethers turned and made their way back to the entrance. Once inside, one of the aliens called DeSoto and reported the conversation he had heard. DeSoto told them to go to Austin Burrow's house and find any information on the substance he sought or information on people or locations Austin had of Arkansas.

The two Nethers once again exited the club, but this time could see no trace of the men. Then walking to their vehicle, they stepped inside the car and brought up a 3 - dimensional image on their GPS device. They looked at the address of Austin Burrows and then pulled out of the parking lot.

The house was a gloomy dilapidated bundle of aged wood, and neither of the Nethers liked the feel or the smell of the house but entering from the front door, they could access it quickly enough. Hearing no physical presence from anyone or having resistance from any humans, they casually walked through the living room as one of the Nethers ascended the stairs up to the rooms on the top floor.

Returning downstairs, the Nether, who had been upstairs, walked up to the other and presented some papers. "I think I may have found something here; it shows that Austin was doing business with some brothers in a township called Caddo Gap, Arkansas, located along the Caddo River. The name of the brothers is Carver. Only about one hundred people live in the entire township, so they won't be hard to find."

The second Nether nodded and said, "Contact Siratchik and let him know this information as quickly as possible." Then the Nether walked over to the coffee table and, looking around, bent down and opened a wooden box. A single plastic bag was there. The alien picked up the bag of Marijuana and eyed it closely, then gently opened and sniffed it, causing him to slightly lurch his head back. He then scanned it with his handheld device, but it was not the substance DeSoto requested, and he tossed it back into the box.

The front door lock was unlatched, then the door was thrown open. Paul walked through the door and glanced at the nether, who was surprised by the stranger's entrance.

Paul eyed the intruder and yelled, "What the fuck?" as he lunged for and grabbed the Nether by the shoulders, intent on doing great bodily harm to this home invader. The Nether changed to a shadow effect, but the giant's grip on him held him fast as the large man pulled him toward him in a giant body hug that completely took his breath from his chest. Just as the Nether felt he would be rendered unconscious, the massive human's eyes went wide then rolled upward as the second Nether struck him from behind hard against his head, knocking Paul out cold.

The two Nethers gathered their things and walked out of the front door toward their vehicle. The Nether, who had been grabbed, rubbed his neck and slid into the car as the other Nether called De Soto and reported the information he had found.

Chapter 10 - Tell No Lies

Sometimes, people, as they do, embellish a story. To gain favor or money or protect someone. It's usually in the form of a little white lie. And some people lie all the time. If their mouth is moving, they're lying. Charlio was one of these. A liar, a thief, and a criminal.

First National Bank off Main Street Miami was loaded with activity. Couples were looking for a home loan, a businessperson securing a business loan, the ordinary person going in, leaving after making a deposit or a withdrawal. And the money flowed through the building as the activity amplified. Charlio and two cohorts were positioned not to rob the bank in the conventional sense but in a roundabout way.

Charlio had one of his men positioned out front who wore an FDOT vest and directed traffic away from some areas of the street and bank, looking every bit a Florida Department of Transportation worker.

Foot and vehicle traffic moved to and from and obeyed his every command. While inside the bank, Charlio and his other man, dressed in city employee garb, worked inside assisting an assistant manager with a supposed maintenance problem while helping themselves to thousands of dollars being transferred to the vault. On the surface, it looked like it may have worked had they been casually able to walk out the entrance, but stupidly has a way of throwing a monkey wrench into every lousy plan.

On the way into the Bank, one of the tellers whose brother worked for the city maintenance office recognized the uniform that Charlio and his associate wore. They knew they were incorrect and alerted the manager of the possible deception. The manager, in turn, contacted city maintenance, who confirmed they did not have any workers scheduled for that building that day. Though their forged papers looked very convincing, Charlio and his men failed to research that the particular uniform was retired and hadn't been worn for some time.

The thrift shop Charlio bought them from failed to mention that fact. Upon leaving the door's exit, they couldn't see their third man anywhere or the four burly police swat officers standing on each side of the doors holding M-16 rifles aimed at anyone exiting. They were quickly arrested and taken to the van holding their third associate. Charlio only kept his head down, not saying a word.

When Zak drove into Miami, he knew he wanted to follow up on the Herb Kershaw lead and felt the best way to start would be to contact the local police. Before doing that, he had to eat.

Zak drove into a familiar burger joint, and the big sign flashed, buy one burger get one free. "That'll work," he thought. I'll save the other for later. But as he exited the joints parking lot, on the corner facing traffic, was a young woman looking a little ragged with the usual cardboard sign imploring for help. And she held a midsize black and white dog on a leash. Zak noticed the dog; first, it looked almost identical to his cousin Seth's dog, Max, when he was little more than a pup.

"Are you hungry?" Zak asked her as his window came down. "YES," she immediately answered as he reached over and grabbed one of the sandwiches and handed it to her, then asked, "Need water." "Sure," she said as Zak gave her a bottle. Then as he rolled up his window, he sped out into the traffic and headed to the police station shown on his GPS.

Although it's only a forty-five-minute drive to Miami, Florida City appears more of an agricultural community.

With a Southern country feel. At the same time, Miami struck Zak as being Metropolitan, more Modern, and sophisticated.

As Zak drove onto the parking lot, the police station highly reflected this. Entering the main building, Zak approached the officer at the admissions desk. Hello officer, I'm Zak Thomas with Homeland Security," Zak showed him the badge provided by the agency. "I'd like to speak with the officer handling the Herb Kershaw case," Zak said, taking back his I.D. and looking over the lobby.

Typing information into his computer, the officer responded, "That would be Detective Mike Rafferty. I'll see if he's available," and then proceeded to call on the desk telephone.

"He'll be down in a few minutes if you want to take a seat over there," the officer stated as he motioned Zak to the waiting area.

Within ten minutes, a forty-ish, well-seasoned law enforcement-looking man came into the lobby and asked the attending officer to point Zak out, then walked over to Zak and extended his right hand. "Mike Rafferty, Miami PD, "Your Zak Thomas with Homeland Security?" the detective asked.

Zak was starting to feel a little uncomfortable with the Homeland Security cover the agency had given him to use in this mission, especially when he had to lie to a detective. Still, he figured the Colonial must have that part covered.

"I am," Zak responded. "Detective Rafferty, would you mind if I ask you a few questions about Herb Kershaw?" "Sure, follow me," Rafferty answered as the two walked down a hall to a waiting area. "You're in luck. We have one of Kershaw's associates in custody that we're holding on a bank robbery charge," he added.

Feeling a bit intrigued, Zak asked, "Detective, would you mind if I speak with that person before you and I speak?" "I suppose that's ok, just let me check on your credentials, and I'll have him sent to a room for you. His name is Charlie Jaun Perez. He goes by Charlio." "That would be great," Zak said as he handed the detective his home security ID card.

"Detective Rafferty returned within twenty minutes and, walking up to Zak, handed him his ID card back. "Well, you check out ok. Follow me. I've got a room all set up for you." Zak and Rafferty walked down the hall until they came to a room facing south. Rafferty pointed to the room and said, "This is our interrogation room. He's all yours. Let me know when you're through. Just speak up when you're ready to end. We'll hear you. Zak hesitated a moment, knowing they would be listening to everything being said, then, grabbing the door handle, walked into the room.

The room looked like dozens of previous rooms he had been in before used for interrogations, all metal, nothing wooden. And on one side of the metal table sat a mid-thirties, Latin-looking man, probably Cuban, Zak thought. The man was intensely focused on the wall to his left and briefly glanced at Zak when Zak entered and sat in a chair across the table and then again focused his attention on the wall left of him.

Zak waited almost an entire half a minute before he spoke. "I'm Zak Thomas, with Homeland Security," (there was that lie again), and I'm here to ask you about Herb

Kershaw." No response. I know you two were associates and did business together. No response. "I'm going to ask you a few questions, then I'm out of your hair," Zak said firmly. No reaction as Charlio burned a hole into the wall with his stare. "Alright, don't talk to me. But you'll have to talk to me once they charge you with Kershaw's murder," Zak said, rising from the chair.

Charlio's head snapped around, looking up at Zak. "THAT'S BULLSHIT," Charlio shouted. "It may be," Zak said, easing back down into the chair, "But that's my recommendation unless you talk to me." "Fuck, that's not how this works," Charlio, now visibly shaken, said back less loudly. "I want a lawyer pronto," he added. "Dude, do you know who I am," Zak said as he moved forward, and his eyes pierced Charlio with their intensity. That move unnerved Charlio badly.

"I am Homeland Security, and I have the full weight of our nation's law enforcement behind me. You do not want to be my enemy," Zak added. Charlio stared at Zak and saw he meant every word and nearly lost his shit. "Yes, me and herb were business partners, but I didn't kill him. I don't know who did, Charlio said with conviction. "When was the last time you saw him?" Zak asked. Zak continued to stare, and Charlio didn't answer for a few seconds as he stared back into Zak's face. "I saw him the night before he was killed, I swear," Charlio pleaded.

"I heard that you and an associate beat up a man named Austin Burrows pretty badly last year," Zak said. "No, no, not badly. We just roughed him up some," Charlio said, then shifted in his chair as he relaxed. "Why did you rough him up?" Zak pressed. "Because the prick was trying to welch on a loan we gave him," Charlio responded. "A loan, for what?" Zak pressed again. "This idiot was always running scams, and he had one in Arkansas, of all places. Austin knew some guys from that area who made homemade Whisky and wanted to buy a large batch and sell it out of the bar under the table. But he never did it, took the money, and used it for himself," Charlio answered. "How much was the loan?" Zak asked, "Thirty Thousand," Charlie answered back. "Why did you and Kershaw loan Austin the money if he was a scammer?" Zak said, himself relaxing a bit with their conversation falling into a more relaxed manner. "We wanted to share in the profits," Charlio said, looking around the room. "But it never happened, and Herb ended up working out an arrangement with Austin.

Hey, I thought you would just ask me a few questions?" Charlio said, now starting to get a little agitated. "Just one more," Zak said. "Do you know who Austin was working with within Arkansas? "Well, I don't think I should answer that," Charlio defiantly answered. Zak leaned in a little closer and said quietly, "Remember, I control your fate." "They're called the Carver brothers," Charlio said, then added, "Are we done? "I'm not on the hook for Kershaw, right?" "No, you didn't kill him. You're clear there. Zak said as he started to leave, "But you're in big trouble for bank robbery." Charlio just sat there with his mouth open as Zak shut the door behind him.

As he exited the room and made his way down the hall, detective Rafferty joined him and said, "Looks like he turned out to be a singer, thanks for the help. That gives me a couple of leads to follow as well. By the way, what is your organization's interest in this case anyway, Thomas? Sorry detective, it's National security. Thanks for all your help. I will call you later if I have any questions?" Zak said as he reached into his pocket for his cell phone. "That's fine," the detective said, and then Zak left Rafferty and headed to the lobby.

Dialing Captain Hiller's number on his phone, he thought, "I better let Chuck know what's going on and bring him up to speed.

Chapter 11 – Making contact with the four soldiers from 1972

When Zak called Hiller to talk to him about Charlio, Zak told him he had a lead on a couple of brothers in Arkansas and was going to drive there and check them out. Zak also asked him what he had discovered about the green substance on Austin's eye.

Hiller told him nothing new, the same thing the doctor had told him, and that's all he knew at that point. Hiller said, "While you're driving to Arkansas, I'll set up an appointment for you to meet up with the four missing soldiers we are keeping at Little Rock Air Force Base." Zak replied, "I should be there in a few days. See if I can meet them around fifteen hundred hours the day after tomorrow." Hiller told him he would have everything arranged for him to meet them when he arrived.

Zak had an uneventful drive from Miami to Little Rock, Arkansas, but sometimes he liked being alone because it gave him time to think and reflect on things.

When Zak arrived, Hiller met him at the building, "Safe drive?" he asked. Zak replied, "Yes, it was good." Before they went inside to see the soldiers, he briefed Zak on what they had found about the three male and one female soldier. He told Zak the soldiers appeared confused about why they were being held captive instead of being let go so they could be reunited with their families.

Walking through the door leading to the room, Hiller said, "Oh, by the way, I have the appointment set up for you to meet the nine-year-old returnee at Area Fifty-One. The meeting is in two days at thirteen hundred hours. I have you cleared to enter the base, so all you have to do is show your credentials when you get to the gate." Zak said, "That will work great. I heard it was hard to get into that place. It will also be interesting to hear that kid's perspective on what happened to him while he was gone."

Once inside the building, all eyes were on him, so Zak conducted himself like a military officer when he met the four soldiers sitting at a long dark brown table. Although Zak is likable, he sat in front of the four soldiers and formally said, "Hi everyone, my name is Zak Thomas, and I'm with Homeland Security. I appreciate all of you meeting with me today. I know you have gone through a lot in your long journey to get back here. My job is to take time with you and see if something in your story was missing when you talked to the other officers. I have some questions that maybe they didn't ask you. By us talking, maybe I can jog your memory about your time away. I must formulate my opinion about what happened to you, not just what I've been told. Does that sound ok with all of you?" Everyone nodded yes, although there seemed to be some doubts on their faces.

One of the soldiers spoke up and said, "But Sir, we've already told the commanding officers everything we can remember." Zak said, "You can call me Zak. You don't need to call me sir." Zak leaned in toward them and, in a quiet voice, said, "I'm a little different kind of military person than the ones you've been talking to since you've been here. The military only sends me to talk to people about a special mission such as supernatural or alien encounters." The four had all their eyes glued to him when the soldier spoke again and said, "Zak, we are not aliens or anything supernatural." Zak said, "The truth is I don't know what you are or what happened to you soldiers. You have been gone a long time. You show up here after being gone for over fifty years. The problem is that everyone claims you have not aged since you have been gone. I need to know how that is possible, and I also need to know where you've been during your time away. "I'm on a mission right now that has brought me here to Arkansas, and in the process, I get to meet and talk to you folks. I don't know yet, but I believe what has brought me here to Arkansas is alien in nature."

The four soldiers looked at each other a little confused, and one finally spoke up and said, "Zak, my name is John Talbert. We are very much American soldiers and not aliens or some type of supernatural person, so why would you want to talk to us about aliens? We know nothing about aliens or the supernatural, so all that is new information to us."

Zak replied, "You don't appear alien to me, John. I've been around aliens for a few years, and I know none of you appear to have their characteristics. But once you know how to identify them, they have an undeniable look and way of talking. "I'm on a mission right now that has brought me here to Arkansas, and in the process, I've been ordered to meet and talk to you soldiers. What brought me here is a possible rogue alien, very dangerous and extremely elusive. I was hoping that you might be able to help me in my hunt to find this alien from another planet. We believe he has killed several people in the Miami area."

John said, "Why would an alien from, as you say, another planet be interested in coming to Earth and killing people?" Zak replied, "He is searching for the ingredients in a formula believed to help keep people young. People have been trying for hundreds of years to find a way to extend their lives, and some have spent their entire life looking for that elusive dream. It is believed there is a mystical place where the formula is derived, and many call that place, "The Fountain of Youth." You may have heard the stories regarding its mystery."

John said, "Yes, we've all heard the stories about the Fountain of Youth, but what does any of that have to do with us? Why would you want to talk to us about the chemical makeup or formula used to extend life? We don't know anything about that."

Zak took a slow look at the four of them and said, "Ok, take a look at it from my perspective, and also take a look at the dilemma that the military and myself are having. The four of you have been missing for fifty years, disappearing in nineteen seventy-two. Thousands of people searched for you when you went missing but couldn't find any traces of you: no uniforms, no weapons, nothing. The search went on for months, even years, and nothing.

Four of you suddenly show up several weeks ago, as if you had just gone missing yesterday. Here is the kicker with everything, none of you have aged during the fifty years you were gone. It is said that you look the same as you did fifty years ago. My question to you is, how is that possible? Many believe that the chemicals and formula for staying young are right here in Arkansas. Don't you think your sudden appearance here in Arkansas raises questions about the possibility of extended life? Especially since you were last seen in Alaska and showed up here in Arkansas. And how did you get here? Did you come on a vehicle or plane, or did you come through a portal? You see my dilemma?"

John said, "We understand why you would have questions that our discovery has created, but we aren't completely sure of the reason we didn't age. They told us that the year is now two thousand twenty-two. Is that true?" Zak said, "Yes, I'm afraid that is true." John replied, "We feel like we've only been gone a week or two."

Zak could detect in John's shaky voice that he wasn't sincere as he said, "John, there are some things you soldiers are not telling me. If you want me to help you, the four of you must come forth with the truth about your disappearance and where you have been."

"Here are my questions for all of you to consider: Were you abducted and held by aliens? Have you been time-traveling through space the entire time? Have you lived in another dimension and teleported back here? If your answer to those questions is no, then I want to know if you had access to the life-sustaining substance that kept you young the entire time you were gone. It seems like a mystery, but it would explain everything to me if you had access to the substance while you were gone."

John reluctantly spoke up again and said, "Zak, the four of us have talked among ourselves after speaking to the other officers, and we are having a problem with all of this. We believed we had only been gone a short period, and now everyone says we are fifty years older. And yes, we reappeared in another state from where we disappeared. We are just as confused about all of that and can't give you an answer to those questions ourselves. It's like we have been in some time warp, or our memory was partially erased. I'm not sure we have the answers that will help anyone."

Seeing that John was willing to talk to him about things, Zak said, "Ok, John, I understand how you must feel, so why don't you take a deep breath and start from the beginning of what you can remember about when you became lost in Alaska in nineteen seventy-two." John took a few deep breaths and said, "We were initially a six-member squad, four men and two women, when we were dropped off in that Alaska area on our mission to find the plane and its passengers. We spent days looking for the downed plane and passengers without any success. At one point, we became lost. We were found by several little people that were about half our size. They had their language, but they talked to us through mind communication or telepathy. They led us into a deep cave under Mt. Hayes in Alaska.

Once there, something happened to us. It was like the mountain walls were pulsating and opened up into some kind of portal; the next thing we knew, we were in another realm or dimension. We were just standing there with the little people, so we asked them what had happened and where we were. They said we had been transferred into paradise through a portal and were safe in this location with them. The place was like the stories you hear about the Garden of Eden. Everything was beautiful and lush green. After a few days, we were transported through a portal to another peaceful place with another group of people they called the Nethers. They served us food, drinks, and bedding. Everything was easy there, and the little people were good to us, treating us exceptionally well before going back to their dimension.

A few other people there looked like us, and we became friends with them. They told us they had been there for years. They told us since being there, they had never aged because of something in the food and the water they were drinking. They didn't know which, or maybe it was both. Those people believed they had eternal life and never wanted to leave. Two members liked the peaceful, loving atmosphere there so much that they wanted to stay. The four of us never wanted to stay. We wanted to complete our mission and go home.

We wanted desperately to get back to our families and our lives. We pleaded with the elders and told them we wanted to return home. Soon, we thought. He told us that it would be ok with their people. He told us they would teleport us to Arkansas to avoid bringing any attention to their home base portal under Mt Hays. We didn't tell this story to any other military soldiers because we promised to keep it a secret. We told them we wouldn't share information about their portal or its location. We also didn't realize we had been with them for fifty years. We find all our families are fifty years older or dead, which disappoints us."

Zak said, "It sounds like the little people and the Nethers had a lot of powers and the ability to go from one portal to another and from dimension to dimension through some type of teleportation. Do you know anything about the chemical they used in the food or drinks that kept you young?" John replied, "No, we never tried to find out anything like that because when we were with them, it never became something of interest to us because we didn't think about staying with them or even about our mortality." At that moment, one of the other soldiers chimed in and said, "Hi Zak, I'm Jerry Burns. Since the military keeps us here, does it mean we're still on active duty? Does that mean we get back pay for the last fifty years?" Jerry said with a big broad smile. Zak chuckled, smiled back, and said, "I don't know what the military has planned for you in that regard, but that is a good point to bring up to our superiors."

Then his manner turned serious again, "Why don't the four of you get together and figure out what you want the Military to do with you? You've lost a lot after fifty years, but at least you have a place to stay until we can all figure out what should happen to you. John said, "Do you know what will happen to us, Zak? We are terrified we might be stuck here for a long time and treated like test animals?" To reassure them, Zak said, "They can't keep you captive forever. I'll see what I can do to help you get out of here, but you need to start thinking about where you would like to go once they set you free, but remember you are still United States Military soldiers."

Zak stood up, shook their hands, and thanked them for being honest with him. Zak had found the answer regarding the life-sustaining chemicals the Nethers and little people used. He didn't know where it came from or how they got them.

He wondered if the rogue alien would try to find the secret of the chemicals for the extension of life from the four soldiers. Before he left, Zak said, "Listen, don't tell that story you just told me to anyone else, or it could get you killed by the rogue alien I'm hunting."

After Zak had left the room, the four soldiers sat bewildered and questioning now what would be their fate. Zak's presence had given them a bit more confidence knowing that he genuinely believed them. They were highly trained, loyal US military soldiers and didn't display any panic or mutiny with their situation. They hoped they hadn't given Zak too much information and it could be used against them.

The room was deathly quiet, and the four soldiers were deep in their thoughts when suddenly the door was abruptly open, and an airman walked in. "Will, you soldiers, come with me?" he commanded.

The soldiers immediately did as they were told and filed out of the room, followed by the Airman who briskly passed in front of them and, walking at a fast pace, motioned them to a large hanger adjoined to the smaller building.

Passing through the open hangar door, they could see the massive area devoid of any aircraft and a detail of twelve men near the center. The Airman motioned the four soldiers to the detail and asked them to follow him. When they approached the detail, the Airman fell off and made his exit.

An older-looking, gruff soldier turned to face them. I am Master Gunnery Sergeant Robert "Buzz" Adams with the 1st Battalion Army Rangers. I have been dispatched from headquarters for your assistance and security until we can transfer you to the Battalion headquarters at Hunters Airfield. Now, if you will come with my men and me, I'll show you to your new living quarters for the time being.

Chapter 12 - The Impersonator

DeSoto was crafty and had mastered one of the arts the Nethers possessed, the ability to cloak their entire body in an invisible outer layer. The technology utilized was three-dimensional hologram imagery surrounding the individual wearer and undetectable to anyone looking around the person wearing the device. Once it was used, they could appear to be a completely different person instead of who they were. Zak knew the Nethers had many advanced technologies, not of this Earth. Soon he would find out just how valuable that power was for DeSoto.

It was mid-morning Friday when a staunch clean-cut, well-dressed Army Major made his way into the Little Rock Air Force Base. His clothes looked as though they had just been pressed, and his shoes were spit-shined to a high gloss. He didn't have any visible weapon to be seen as he confidently found his way to the Base Headquarters. He told the Commanding Officer his name was Major Franklin Kinkade and that the General had commissioned him to have a meeting with the four soldiers they were detaining. He presented the commanding officer with fake paperwork stating his name and purpose. The C.O. looked them over and then questioned Kinkade intensely, but the Major had answers for all the questions he was being asked.

After a few minutes, Kinkade quietly said, "Sir, can you set me up a few minutes to talk to these four people? It is vitally important to the security of the United States that I talk with them immediately." When he said that, the C.O. raised his head and looked at Kinkade directly. "Can I ask you what purpose, maybe?" Kinkade said, "I'm not at liberty to discuss matters with anyone except the General." The C.O. could see that the Major was someone not to be taken lightly. With little hesitation, he informed Kinkade he would allow the Major to speak to them.

He called one of the Lieutenants over and told him to inform the soldiers that a United States Major was there to talk to them. The Lieutenant immediately left headquarters and headed to the building where the soldiers were being kept. He then returned and told the C.O. the soldiers were being sent to the orderly room where the Major could speak to them under supervision. The Major said, "Thank you, Lieutenant. I appreciate your help." He replied, "I will walk you over to the room and wait for you while you talk to them." Kinkade said, "That will be fine, thank you."

When the soldiers entered the room, Major Kinkade and the Lieutenant were standing by the large table where they would sit. The soldiers stood at attention and gave the Major a salute. He returned their salute and said, "At ease, soldiers." He motioned for them to sit at the table as he and the Lieutenant took their seats.

He started speaking as he introduced himself and told the soldiers the General had sent him to talk to them about their experience while they were gone for fifty years. He asked the soldiers what they thought may have happened and why they had not aged the entire time.

Forgetting what Zak had told them about not talking to anyone else about their story, John Talbert slowly spoke up and said, "I will speak for myself and the rest of this group." Kinkade softly said, "Great, John, we just want to find answers to some crucial questions. Was another race of people keeping you while you were gone, maybe of alien heritage?" John replied, "By the little people and the Neither's." Yes, they were both an alien race and one from another planet." Did you know you were being given algae or substance in your water or food?" asked Kinkade. John looked at the other soldiers, saying, "We didn't know at first, but we found out later they were giving us something in our water supply. When we realized we weren't aging, we asked some individuals we had become friends with what it was and where it came from." Kinkade almost couldn't wait as he interrupted and said, "Where was it from, and what was in it, do you know?"

John was starting to get a little suspicious about Kinkade's questions but continued, they told us it was an algae they mixed with the water that had some kind of chemicals in it, but we didn't know anything about any of the ingredients. The algae were supposed to be from a remote area in the Ozarks of Arkansas. It was around Glenwood, Arkansas, and a little town with a strange name. That's all we know about the substance; we don't even know how it all works." Kinkade asked several more questions, but they were unimportant because he already had all the necessary information.

He thanked the four soldiers for their time and thanked the Lieutenant for sitting in on the meeting with him. They all saluted each other as they quickly made their exits.

Once off the base, DeSoto uncloaked the holographic device. He whispered, "That worked well, and I have what I was looking to retrieve. That little town in Arkansas is the key to the algae and water substance; I'm sure I'll find it there. When I find this substance, it'll make me rich. Plus, I will live forever."

Chapter 13 – Meeting with Truman Wallace

Hiller went with Zak to where Truman was being held at a military-safe house in Area Fifty-One, deep inside the Nevada desert. Scientists, psychiatrists, and other top U.S. officials were interviewing Truman since his return and after his parents returned him to the military.

Zak told Hiller, "Why don't you wait outside and let me see if I can get a feel for this kid?" Hiller replied, "that is a good idea. I'll wait for you out here in the next room." Zak went into a well-guarded room and sat at a table, waiting for Truman to arrive with his escorts. Two highly trained military police walked him in and sat him at the table. He wasn't cuffed or restrained in any way.

When the boy first walked in, Zak was somewhat taken aback. He looked no different to Zak than all the other nine-year-old kids his age. He was of medium height and built with well-trimmed light brown hair. The military had him dressed in current and modern clothing and wearing shined shoes.

He was introduced to Zak, and they shook hands and sat at the table across from each other. He was very polite and seemed pleasant enough for the two to converse with each other based on his easy disposition. However, he did seem somewhat apprehensive about being questioned again.

After the two guards stepped out, Zak started having a light conversation with him about his likes and dislikes and his family. He told Zak he was a little mixed up about his family because, after his return, he had stayed a short time with people the military said were his family, but they said they were not his mother and father. Truman told Zak those people were a lot older than his birth parents. He said they didn't want him staying with them. He also said they didn't look like what he remembered because they had aged so much.

Zak said, "I know you have been interviewed a few times in the last months or so, but I want you to know I want to talk to you for an entirely different reason than everyone else has talked to you about." The boy looked up from the table and met Zak's eyes. "What do you mean, he asked?" Zak leaned forward and whispered, "This is a secret between you and me. You can't tell anyone else what I'm going to say to you." Now Zak had Truman's full attention as Truman leaned forward and said, "Sure, you can trust me. I won't tell anyone. They won't let me talk to anyone anyway."

Zak continued to whisper, "I hunt aliens from other planets, but I hunt the ones that want to cause harm to us here on Earth. I don't bother the good aliens like the Sungcut or little people in the Triangle and the Nethers from another dimension. Those are good aliens from good dimensions." Zak had already assumed that if the Sungcut had abducted Truman when he was a boy and released him twenty-five years later without aging, they had to be aware of some type of alien powers.

Truman couldn't believe someone else might think about what had happened to him. He asked Zak, "How do you know all this about the Sungcut people?" Zak said, "I've traveled to different dimensions and planets, and I'm friends with the aliens on those planets. I know they are honest and also a peace-loving race. But they are just like people here on Earth. Some bad ones decide they want fame or fortune and try to hurt others to get something they want. Such is the case with a rogue alien from Nether I'm hunting.

I'm looking for him right now. He killed several people in Florida trying to find a substance that is supposed to give people extended life. Do you understand what I mean by extended life? Truman shook his head yes, up and down. "The guy I'm hunting is selfish and wants to have that substance all to himself so he can live forever, get rich and use it to gain eternal power. He will kill anyone, including you, to get the information he wants." Truman's eyes widened, and he said, "Why would he want to kill me? I don't know anything about any of that extended life stuff."

Zak said, "It doesn't matter. He will force it out of you if he thinks you know anything about it."

Zak had a funny feeling this kid knew much more than he was telling him or what he had told the other military personnel. He decided he would try a different approach with him. He looked Truman in the eyes and said very slowly, "You lived somewhere for twenty-five years, Truman, and during that time, you never got any older. You're still only a nine-year-old boy. We believe the people you were with, the Sungcut (Little People), Nethers, or whatever you want to call them, gave you something in your food and water to keep you young. If that's not true, you traveled throughout space for twenty-five years and then returned to the same place you were twenty-five years ago.

That is why your parents didn't believe the story about you. They knew you should be thirty-four years old and not nine as you were when they last saw you. They didn't think it was you. They believed you were a clone, robot, or something else the government had produced to try and fool them." Truman said, "I wondered why they didn't keep me."

"What do you think happened to you when you were gone? Do you even know, or are you trying to protect, the Sungcut people or someone else? Remember, I'm a good guy, and I'm just trying to catch the alien killer before he kills too many more people, including you. You may not even be safe here with all this protection. If that alien wants to find you, he will get the information he wants from you. He can be sneaky in getting to his victims."

Truman acted as though he had to trust someone, and Zak seemed honest to him. He also didn't want to get killed by someone trying to find the existence of some life-extending substance. Truman told Zak that the leader of the little people was a good example to all his people. He taught them to hide from the earthlings and disappear into another dimension when people got too close. He said, "The Sungcut people have exceptional strength and speed to avoid capture."

After a few months with the little people, they took me to live with a race of people in another dimension that looked just like Earthlings. They were known as the Nethers. The entire time I was gone, I continued to ask them to return me to my parents. The Nethers were good to me and treated me like their son. I lived in a comfortable and pleasant environment as if I were one of them. Over some time, I did find that I was not aging. I asked some of the elders why not, and they told me the Nethers had found a substance on Earth that, when mixed with local water and algae from that area, could extend life for hundreds of years. It was said that the substance was made available to the Nether people in their drinking water in a diluted state. I was also told they also passed on the substance to the Sungcut people because they were also an alien race and peaceful to the Nethers."

Zak thought, "This kid doesn't sound like a nine-year-old boy anymore. He sounds more like that thirty-four-old and the age he was supposed to be."

The Nethers took good care of me but finally gave in to my wishes to be with my family and agreed to release me back to the Sungcut people. Once the little people agreed, they released me back to where I had disappeared. They tried to wipe my memory clean about my time with them. They used some mind control over me while I was with them. I still have some bits and pieces of images of living with their people." Zak thought, "That is weird. They could've done it easily if they wanted to clean his memory."

Zak was having a little bit of a hard time believing everything Truman was telling him. He didn't understand why they would suddenly decide to let him go and return him to his parents. He said, "Can you give me some ideas of what your life was like and how you were treated while you were gone? Truman replied, "When the Sungcut people first took me, I didn't understand why they kept me in the first place. Why not just return me to the woods where I became lost? I was upset with them for not taking me back. They told me they would give me a better place to live than where I was living with my parents. While I was with them, I lived in a large building with high walls all around. The people were all loving and caring toward me. They treated me like I was one of their family. It was peaceful and loving, and there were a lot of other kids my age to play with and hang around. I can't give you much detail about everything. That's just some of the bits and pieces that I can remember now."

Zak's mind momentarily drifted away as he thought, "I wonder why they decided to let Truman return after all the time they held him captive. Maybe time didn't mean anything to them with the age substance they were taking. It might have been like time was standing still for them. Maybe they thought if he realized he had not aged and his family was all gone, he would return to them. Or maybe there was another reason."

He snapped back to Truman and said, "I don't want to scare you, but if that alien I'm looking for finds out what you just told me, he may torture you or kill you to get the information he wants from you, and especially what you just told me. Once he knows this information, he will attack the Sungcut people and kill as many of them as possible to get his hands on that Substance. Do the Sungcut people have any type of weapons to protect themselves?" Truman's eyes widened, visibly upset as he replied, "I don't want anything to happen to any of those people. They are too kind and loving to try and hurt.

They have weapons, but I don't know what type they have. They have the same type as the Nethers. They are all close friends with each other. Zak said, "That's good because they may need to use them against this rogue alien if I can't stop him." Truman asked, "What is the name of the rogue Nether that has killed the people in Florida?" Zak said I'm not sure what his identity is, but I'll find out."

Zak's thoughts temporarily drifted back again to the story about the Sungcut hunters that killed the Caribou in the Forrest. "They probably shot it with a hand-held energy-directed weapon, which would explain why there was no loud sound from a rifle firing. Explaining why the herd of Caribou had not run off."

Zak thanked him for his honesty and told him not to worry. He was going to have additional security watch out for him. He told Truman not to talk to anyone about what he had told him and to let him know if someone tried getting in to see him or began pressuring him for answers.

He called Chuck over and said, "I'll fill you in on everything once we leave, but we need to talk to the officers to put on extra guards to watch over this kid. We need to tell them not to let anyone else talk to him unless they have our approval."

Chapter 14 – DeSoto and the Sungcut people

Taking a minute to talk to his comrades, DeSoto said, "Meet me at the coordinates I'm going to send to you. It's in the wilderness of Alaska. I'll meet you there and give you further instructions," DeSoto told his comrade through one of two satellite telephones he had acquired. Earth technology, he felt, was primitive but valuable here on this planet.

"Why are we chasing these people and locations around this globe, Siratchik? Why don't we abduct one of the scientists on Nether and force the formula from them, or better yet, replicate the formula in a lab of our design," the comrade quizzed.

"No! We can't do either. First, the fallout from taking a high-level science technician would bring down too much suspicion and heat on my motives. And replication? It can't be done. The formula will not be successful unless the ingredient is sourced from the original water and algae, which I do not have.

Just do what I say, and you'll be paid very well," DeSoto stressed. "In Gold?" the comrade asked. "In Gold!" DeSoto said, "Used anywhere across the Universe," he added.

It was early morning, and the sun had just begun to shine through the trees as three small hunters skillfully hunted for their Caribou prey. They had been on the herd's trail for a while when they noticed a strange craft parked only a few miles away. One of the hunters spoke in their language and said that they should look at it and see what it was doing in the middle of the wilderness. Maybe find out where this race belonged.

They had seen craft before but usually flew at tremendous speeds to reach their destinations and never stopped. Never had they seen one parked and so close to the entrances to their extraordinary caves.

The craft was circular in dimensions and had a silver color that reflected light like the sun shining on a smooth lake. Three legs supported it in a triangle about ten feet off the ground. A doorway with stairs led to the ground, and the door was open. The three hunters hid behind trees and large rocks and made their way within forty yards of the craft. It sat silently, not making any sound or movement.

One hunter looked over at the two other hunters and asked what they thought it was doing there. They just shrugged, I don't know, as they circled the craft. One of the hunters picked up a rock, threw it, and hit the craft, but there was no reaction from within. They did that again, and still no answer from inside the ship.

Since Sungcut people have enormous speed and strength, one of the Sungcuts motioned for another to run up to the ship entrance and look inside. He followed the order and did it so quickly that it was like watching a shadow move at lightning speed. He looked inside and yelled back to the other hunters that it was empty. Being empty, they knew the occupants were nearby in the woods.

At that time, DeSoto and his two comrades came out of hiding and approached the three hunters from different directions. Their weapons were drawn and ready to fire if they had to use them for self-defense. At first, the three Sungcuts instantly jumped behind rocks, and DeSoto's accomplices fired two warning shots from their energy-directed weapon in their direction. "We are not trying to hit you deliberately," DeSoto yelled. "We are not here to harm you. We would've killed you if we were here to destroy you." None of the three hunters volunteered to return to the open to be seen for the risk of being shot. Also, none of them volunteered to say anything to these three beings that had purposely invaded their hunting territory.

DeSoto yelled again, not getting any response from the three Sungcuts, "We don't want to harm you. We are just here to ask you questions. I want to find out about your water and food sources. We need help on our planet. I am interested in where the water and algae come from and what your people put into it that extends a person's life."

One of the hunters said to the other two, "It's just another Nether species trying to steal our secret. We weren't allowed to give up information regarding the water or food we drank or ate to anyone. That information is sacred, a gift given to us by our ancestors, and we must fight to our death to protect the information. We won't try to kill them with our weapons. Let's try to scare them away."

One of the hunters said, "So what are we going to do?" "We can outrun them, but they will have a way to track or follow us. I'm going to fire two shots from our weapon at their craft and see if that will get their attention. The two of you grab large rocks and start throwing them toward the intruders while I fire the two shots." They nodded in agreement, started looking for rocks to throw, and quickly rounded up two piles of them about the size of softballs. DeSoto was still trying to reason with the Sungcuts, thinking he could get what he wanted by talking to them.

The hunters fired two large explosions that hit beneath the craft. It wasn't enough to destroy or disable it but get DeSoto's attention. At the same time, the other two hunters began throwing seven to eight-pound rocks toward DeSoto's group. The actions of the little people angered DeSoto when he decided there was no talking with them. He was angry that they had hit his ship with two powerful rounds from their weapons. He and his men began to fire where he thought the three little people were located, not knowing how fast they were. He didn't realize they were already in a different location and throwing rocks from those locations. So many stones came in from different directions that DeSoto told his men to take cover and to fire at them to kill.

The three hunters decided to run for cover to escape in their cave. They quickly escaped DeSoto's onslaught and found their way toward the cave entrance. It was only a few miles away. To their surprise, DeSoto and his men didn't give up the chase, as they followed at a safe distance, occasionally taking wild shots at them.

The fighting between the two groups continued for about twenty minutes until the hunters made their way into the cave opening. They fired a couple of times in DeSoto's direction with their weapon, but it still didn't detour his stubborn desire. He was determined to find out whatever he could about the algae and the water, even if DeSoto had to kill a few of the Sungcut people to get what he wanted.

Once inside the massive cave, the three Sungcut's waited for DeSoto and his men to make it close to the entrance, where they could see each other. One hunter waved his hand in a circular motion, and a portal hole opened up for them, and they instantly jumped inside. Once inside, the hole quickly closed behind them, and all that was left were rigid rock walls. Once inside, they were no longer in the Earth realm but a dimension of their own that DeSoto could not penetrate.

DeSoto and his men fired shots into the cave walls, but nothing happened. It was just a solid rock wall. DeSoto had seen those portals before and knew nothing he could do because he wasn't sure what dimension the little people had disappeared into. He also didn't possess the key to opening that portal. He angrily yelled, "I can't believe it, those little Fucker's got away from us."

He spent a couple more days in the forest trying to see if other Sungcut people may return, but none showed, or at least, he never saw them. They were frustrated with the little people. He gave up his search in the forest and went into the small local villages. He told everyone he was a reporter trying to get information about the Sungcut people. From what the locals told him, it seemed like nothing but exaggerated fictional bits and pieces of stories. None of it sounded realistic or convincing, at least nothing that would help him with what he was looking to find.

One tribe leader told him, "If the little people don't want you to find them, you never will. They are not of this Earth; they live in another realm. If you get close to them, they just disappear right before your eyes into that realm." Of course, this was the kind of information that DeSoto knew he couldn't work with if it were true, and he began to realize he would never get the information he needed from the little people.

Hiller called Zak the following day. Once he had him on the phone, he said, "Zak, a couple of witnesses have come forward and reported to the local police a bizarre incident up there in Alaska. Some local hunters said they followed three assailants chasing the little people and firing different weapons at them they weren't familiar seeing before. The witnesses said they didn't believe they were trying to kill them but just trying to get them to stop running. At first, the assailants tried to stop them long enough to talk to them. But the Sungcuts wouldn't stop and went to their caves, and they never saw them again."

Zak was silent for a few minutes as he listened to Hiller. Zak whispered, "So there are three of them now." He asked, "Did the witnesses see a spacecraft?" Hiller replied, "They didn't mention seeing anything like that. They said the three men chased the little people into a cave below Mt. Hayes and the little people disappeared." Zak was already beginning to believe these were the aliens he was after. He also believed DeSoto had already figured out the little people were using the water and the algae. He said, "I think those aliens may be the guys that have something to do with the murders in Florida. I'm starting to see a connection. Nothing I can be specific about yet, but as soon as I figure it out, I'll let you know." Hiller said, "I figured you would be interested in this story because it involved the little people and the Alaskan Triangle." "Exactly," said Zak. "I need to hear anything bizarre like that, no matter where it may happen." Hiller replied, "Ok, we will keep you informed on everything we hear from here on our end." Zak thanked him for the information as they hung up the phone.

Not getting anywhere with the little people, DeSoto decided to focus on a more specific location in Arkansas and possibly a more accessible lead of the local Carver brothers.

Chapter 15 – The Carver Brothers

Orville Carver sat on a large Oak stump that overlooked his family home across the creek. "Ellawisa, she's my gal," he softly sang as he eyed the house. He was afraid to go inside.

Charlie was pissed and ready to fight. Being the older brother and larger and filled out, Charlie was tougher than Orville and could wallop Orville if he wanted. However, Orville could hold his own in a fight. But Charlie had good reason to be pissed. Orville had taken several cases from their Still back in the woods and transported them to a private party organized for their cousin.

Ordinarily, in these parts of Arkansas, everyone is either related or very close friends. But this cousin Charlie hated, having been cheated out of several hundred dollars in the past of sold and not paid for Shine by the cousin. And the worst part about this was Orville was giving them the Whiskey for the affair for free behind Charlie's back.

Orville always was the easier-going brother, and to him, family trumped all. As he said, "Sides, you can't stay mad at someone forever. God bless em!" Orville finally gave in and walked the path down to the front door.

When he entered, Charlie was cleaning his Henry 30/30 rifle, but Orville was undeterred from entering, knowing his brother would never shoot him intentionally. He sat next to his brother, who continued looking at his rifle while vigorously rubbing it with an old oil-stained rag.

"Whatcha doin, Charlie?" Orville meekly asked. Charlie, after a pause, answered, "I'm going back up to the Still." "I've gotta make up for the batch you stole." "Stole?" Orville gasped, "Charlie, theys kin. Ikes gettin married, and that's our weddin present."

Charlie stopped rubbing on the propped-up rifle and stared straight at Orville, "And you think that makes it right?" Charlie angrily asked. "There ain't no reason to get any more worked up. If it makes you feel easier bout it, take the proceeds from my next amount to pay for the shine," Orville said. Charlie exclaimed, "You damn straight I will."

In a lighter tone, Charlie said, "You want to come up with me to the Still." "Yes sir, yes sir, I do, just let me grab my gear," Orville said as he sprang out of his chair and sprinted for his bedroom.

Charlie drove the older model Ford F-150 along the trail out of Caddo Gap and into the hills. Once they reached Buttermilk Creek, they would need to exit the truck and walk the rest of the way up to their secret spot toward Bear Den Hollow.

While the vehicle bounced along the trail, the two didn't speak much. Charlie was still ticked at Orville, who was about ready to bust, but finally broke the silence. "Are you going to the Weddin, Charlie?" Orville asked enthusiastically. "No!" Charlie said, "How bout I get Ike to say he's sorry?" Orville implored. "Screw Ike Dalton and screw his wedding!" Charlie shot back. Orville replied, "Charlie, he's your cousin. Momma and daddy would turn over in their grave to hear you talk that way bout kin," Orville said, feeling a family appeal would help. "Yeah, well, Daddy wouldn't abide no thief, and that is what Ike Dalton is, no matter a cousin."

"Uncle Leeroy may be Momma's brother, but Ike doesn't seem to care less. He still steals from us every chance he gets. I asked him to work for us at the still, but no, he wouldn't hear it. Nothing but a waste of breath," Charlie said, working himself into a slight frenzy. But seeing the sad look on Orville's face, he relented and said, "Ok, bro, I'll represent our Shine and us." Orville smiled broadly. Charlie just looked over at him as he scowled while pulling into the parking area they used next to the creek.

As the men exited the truck, Charlie grabbed his Henry rifle from the gun rack mounted on the inside of the truck cab. Orville grabbed his rifle, an older model Browning twelve-gauge pump shotgun, off the rack. In the distance lay the dense forest with Buttermilk Creek meandering at their side in concert with the surroundings.

The trek to the Still was not long, and the brothers enjoyed the crisp feel of the air that whipped through the trees. When they arrived at the site, they could see it was undisturbed and unmolested by the Dalton boys or the law.

Charlie immediately made for the cooking room and started grabbing various pieces of wood and utensils, jumping right into the work. Orville looked over at Charlie and said, "I'm going to head up with these jugs to get some water from the creek; we need about five to ten gallons to make our brew, be back shortly," and headed further up the creek that was surrounded by the forest.

The Appalachian Mountains are beautiful in the spring and hold a lot of mysteries. The woods are full of healthy growing flora and wild animals. The sounds emitted from the backcountry are always ultra-alive in their intensity as they seem to echo and reverberate. Orville loved the sounds and the forest that he had grown up playing, hunting, and hiding in the thickets.

DeSoto had found out from other moonshiners where Charlie and Orville had their Still and was waiting for them when they arrived. He stayed hidden from sight as he watched their activity. He waited until Orville began walking up the mountain with a large plastic jug in each hand as the other brother worked fervently inside a makeshift shed.

DeSoto moved his hand over a GPS device, which brought up a screen. He then spoke the name Orville Carver into the device and asked for a reference. The machine brought up several images of Orville Carver and then cross-referenced his family, bringing up pictures of his brother, mother, and father. DeSoto pressed the image of Orville's father on the device, which brought up a miniature 3 - dimensional image of the man from all angles.

DeSoto moved to Orville's right, followed him from a safe distance, and saw Orville stop by a running stream and kneel. DeSoto came to the north of the stream and, standing behind a large White Oak, removed his handheld GPS device and affixed it to his wristband.

He then brought up the image of Roland Carver in a small 3 - dimensional state. Then pressing another portion of the GPS device, he locked the image into the imaginator. Then the machine lit to a fine light, and DeSoto passed his right hand over his left wrist, and the 3 - dimensional shape enveloped him, and he stepped out from behind the large Oak as if he were Roland Carver. Inflections, vocals, and mannerisms were superimposed into the image.

Orville heard the voice, subtle at first and then more prominent as it began to irritate him and caused him to turn. It was his name being called, but it wasn't by Charlie. His irritation was that it could be one of the Dalton boys. The voice sounded vaguely similar, but not one of the Dalton's, but familiar. A chill caused his arms to slightly tingle as his senses flexed.

"Hello, son," the voice said as Orville's dad stepped closer to the opening in the dense forest. Orville felt the chill now shoot through his entire upper body as he viewed the figure standing mere yards away. Orville felt his eyes burn as moisture filled them. "Daddy," Orville whispered, "Yous dead." Orville's father smiled and waved, saying, "Hello, Orville," and then turned toward a large White Oak. Orville gasped as he sprinted toward the figure but could only see a shadow as it faded behind the tree.

Orville leaped toward where his father stood but only found the forest's echoing sounds, the soft green underbrush at his feet, and intermittent silence. No father, no ghosts. Orville leaned against the White Oak and yelled out his father's name, "Roland Carver!" and then again more loudly, "Roland Carver!" and then added quietly, "Dad." But the silence was like a tomb, and Orville turned on his heels back toward the jugs, puzzled and sad, and made his short journey back to the Still.

When Orville arrived at the Still, Charlie glanced up from the bucket he was filling and said, "Where are the jugs?" But Orville moved very slowly as he walked with his head down into the Still's shed and sat on a chair made from a stump.

Gripping the shotgun by the pump, he stood it on the ground on end and leaned his head against it with his head down. Charlie walked over and knelt next to Orville. "What's wrong, bro?" Charlie asked while putting his hand on Orville's shoulder. After a pause, Orville lifted his head and said, "I saw Daddy!" Charlie took a moment after staring at Orville and then asked, "Have you been drinking the whiskey again?"

As Orville continued to stare, he shook his head sideways, back and forth, as he looked down. "Not a drop." Of course, he was lying. "He was there by God. Waving and he smiled at me and said my name. But when I called his name, he didn't answer, and then he was gone," Orville slowly said as he stared straight ahead.

Once DeSoto saw Orville's profound reaction to seeing and hearing his father, he realized he had made a mistake and faded behind the woods to reapproach him at another time and location. He had shaken Orville so severely he could never approach him as rattled as he was.

Charlie lifted Orville and shook his shoulders. "You know we've been seeing a lot of crazy shit out here in these woods lately. Man up, bro, now, we have work to do." Then Charlie put his arm around Orville's shoulder as he walked him out of the shed. "Let's go get those jugs," he added. Orville nodded and started walking on his own steam.

They were able to fill the jugs and take them back to the Still and finish brewing their shine. It wasn't long before they picked up their guns and equipment and headed out of the area.

A shadow moved on the other side of the building, and a figure stepped into the light watching the brother's truck taillights disappear down the road into the dense forest. Then DeSoto fully materialized and stepped into the shed.

He looked around his surroundings, knowing his next step would be to meet the brothers face to face and find out what they knew about the algae, water, and its location. Not realizing he was standing not too far from the answers he was seeking.

Chapter 16 – DeSoto Meets the Carver Brothers

The March morning crispness was starting to fade as light rolled into the small town of Caddo Gap. The occasional rim hum of a bicycle tire could be heard as the paper carrier threw the few newspapers delivered in the small city. And the less occasional car rolled down the main street, stopping at the local diner for a coffee before heading to work.

Orville pulled the Ford truck into the back of the small grocery store and unloaded a case of his and Charlie's finest brew. The tall, overweight man, the proprietor, wiped his hands on his white apron to remove any remnants of the sausage he was making before picking up the case and taking it further into his back storeroom. He went to the door and said, "Another batch from that sweet water, I, see?" he said to Orville." "Yes, Sir, we have the best water on the mountain, straight from Buttermilk Creek," Orville said with a big broad grin as he waved goodbye. He was spinning out into the street with his truck as he left. "I won't argue with that," the grocer yelled as he waved goodbye to Orville.

DeSoto standing nearby, walked to the back of the grocery store and slipped through the door leading to the rear storeroom. He slowly walked into the back of the storeroom, looking for the whiskey that Orville had just delivered.

Walking over to the case in the far corner of the room, De Soto picked up one of the jars and walked toward the door.

He lifted the bottle towards the light and examined the bottle's contents, trying to see any irregularities or residual residue floating in the liquid.

The waters of these parts of the Ozarks were known to be extremely high in calcium and magnesium. Many of the whiskeys made with these waters were highly prized for their taste, and people laughed and joked about it being a longevity drink. But the most prized whiskey in the area was that made by the Carver brothers.

Seeing no residue in the bottle, DeSoto lowered his arm and attempted to turn around. "Hey, what the hell are you doing in my storeroom? Set my bottle down, now." The grocer advanced toward DeSoto's back with a large meat cleaver in his hand.

Feeling threatened, DeSoto quickly turned, pulled his Ion gun, and fired a single shot into the grocer's head. He hit him in the dead center in the forehead, knocking him backward and completely lifeless, the cleaver flying to the far side of the room. DeSoto walked over to the dead grocer and said, "You should have left me alone, and you'd still be alive." He turned and walked toward the exit door.

As he walked outside, he saw Orville's Ford truck parked a couple of blocks up the street while Orville was inside the building. DeSoto walked up to the truck, looked into the back, and saw no cases left, just an empty tarp lying in the bed. He slowly and silently slipped into the truck's bed under the tarp. He lay there waiting for Orville to get back into the truck cab, which he did a few minutes later.

Orville lazily headed up the hill towards his family home, and once arriving, he parked the truck to the side, walked up a path, and sat on a big oak stump. He took a swig from a jug of Shine he was carrying and looked down on the family home. Orville thought, "I love this place. It's my home."

While Orville was preoccupied, DeSoto slipped out of the back of the truck bed and hid behind some bushes and trees. He watched to see what Orville was going to do next. After an extended period, Orville finally ambled down the path to the house's front door and walked inside.

DeSoto followed from a distance, not to be seen, and stood on one side of the house as Orville entered. Once inside, Desoto slipped to the side and looked into the open front door. He saw another man, who he believed to be Orville's brother, Charlie, in the room polishing his rifle as Orville sat down next to him and began to converse. Charlie looked angry with Orville, but he said something that made Orville happy.

Orville suddenly jumped up with an excited look and ran for the back of the house. DeSoto slipped back toward the edge of the truck and waited to see if any action would happen before he made a move to meet them.

Within minutes, the screen door burst open, and Orville, carrying several pieces of gear and a shotgun, loaded into the truck's cab. And subsequently, Charlie followed out the door carrying his gear and a rifle. He poured into the cab with his gear, mounted the driver's side, started the engine, and began to pull out into the dirt road.

DeSoto decided this was the opportune time. He stepped out in the open and in front of the Truck. He yelled, "Hello there, are you the Carver brothers?

Charlie stopped the truck dead in its tracks. Charlie and Orville were frozen in time for a brief moment. Orville said, "Hey, how the fuck did that guy get here? I didn't hear a truck or car come up our way?" Charlie said, "Maybe he was already here, hiding and waiting for us? Be careful, Orville."

Charlie got an angry look, and the two brothers bravely got out of the truck and strolled toward DeSoto. When Charlie was within a few feet of him, he got in DeSoto's face and said, "Yes, we're the Carver brothers, but what business is it of yours? Are you one of those County people that's here again to try and lock us up for selling our Shine? If so, you caught us heading to our precious cargo." Charlie was now so close that DeSoto could smell the alcohol that shot out of the mouth at every word Charlie said.

DeSoto was clever as he quickly said, "Heck no, I'm not one of those people. I'm here to see if I can buy a couple of jugs of your whiskey. I heard from people around here that it was some of the best in Arkansas. I was wondering if I could try it for myself. Maybe I could buy a couple of jugs from you?"

Orville's mood suddenly changed to being proud of their shine and popped off and said, "It ain't the best in Arkansas. It's the best in the entire United States. Nobody can make shine as we do." Charlie said, "Shut up, Orville."

Charlie still wasn't convinced if this guy was connected to the law or not, so he was cautious as he carefully eyed DeSoto. He said, "I can tell because of how you're dressed. You ain't from around these parts, so where'd you come from, mister? How did you get here? Did you park your vehicle down the road somewhere?" DeSoto ignored part of Charlie's question as he replied, "I come from a place in California, and nobody makes moonshine there. We have to buy our whiskey in the stores. I want to know why you think your moonshine is much better than any other moonshiners around here."

Orville couldn't help himself as he opened his mouth again and said, "With our shine, you don't wake up with much of a hangover the next day unless you drink a lot of it. And you don't end up all wrinkled up and old after drinking it for many years, like with the others." DeSoto smiled and wanted to hear more. Orville's pride in his shine forced him to continue, "It's all about our water."

Charlie quickly turned around, pulled Orville aside, and whispered, "Don't open your trap one more time about our Shine. You idiot, do you want everybody trying to take our water spot? Make damn sure you don't say anything about the water in Buttermilk Creek or Crawford Brumley."

Orville saw that he pissed Charlie off, so he claimed up and backed away. Charlie went to the truck bed, retrieved two jugs of the shine, and handed them to DeSoto. He collected two hundred dollars from DeSoto and angrily thanked him.

DeSoto was trying to ask questions about the moonshine as Charlie was walking away. Charlie and Orville were in their truck and leaving when Charlie said, "Hey, mister, sorry we can't talk with you anymore, we got deliveries to make, so I hope you enjoy the Shine."

DeSoto decided not to kill Charlie and Orville at that time. He didn't know the source of their water or anything about the algae. He believed it had something to do with the water near their Still that made the difference in the Carver Moonshine. DeSoto knew he had to continue to find out more information from them before he would have the answers to the questions he was searching to find.

Once they left, Orville said, "Where do you suppose that guy came from, Charlie? He just popped up out of nowhere. Like a ghost." Charlie said, "See, I told you some strange stuff was happening around here."

Chapter 17 – Crawford Brumley

If you traveled further up the dirt road from Caddo-Gap, you could only travel about twenty miles upward into the hills on the dirt road before reaching the Ozark Mountains. The old highway was potted with holes and occasional huge rocks that had fallen off the side of some of the hills. The trees further up the canyon were so thick that they completely covered the road, but you could still get a car or pickup through the one-lane road. It was so dark that it would've been scary for an individual if he had to travel that road alone at night.

Off the side of the road, the brush was so thick that deer could be seen grazing only a few feet away. Sometimes you couldn't even see them because of the heavy brush. Occasionally, a rattlesnake would be seen bathing in the sun in the middle of the road. The further you went up the mountains, the more it became desolate. You realized it was just you and a few other people who had ventured that far on that old dusty road.

When you arrived at where the road ended, if you wanted to go further, you had to park your car, get out, and hike the rest of the way. The far less traveled trail led from the road end and went up several more miles into the even more wooded and desolate area. The trail was called the DeSoto

Trail. Along the trail was Buttermilk Creek and the Carver brothers collected water from it for their Still.

Unbeknownst to many local people, it was at the end of the trail that a middle-aged man, Crawford Brumley, had decided to make the land his home. He had lived alone for many years. He appeared to be in his fifties but good physical shape. He looked as though he was capable of taking care of himself if he got into a physical brawl with someone. He lived in an old weather-torn cabin that had been there for over one hundred years. The place had never been painted, so it looked even older and more run-down than it was.

Crawford had very few visitors and didn't welcome many on his property. He had signs tacked up on trees to keep out of his property. They said, "Stay out. Trespassers will be killed." That was enough to discourage most people from venturing onto his land. He was a loner and liked being left alone. He had plenty of weapons for protection and two healthy Blue Tick Hounds, as his best friends, a male, and a female, for his added protection. They let Crawford know when anyone stepped foot on or was near the property.

Crawford Brumley built the Cabin in his mid-fifties after the makeshift cabin he lived in was hit by lightning and burned to the ground. None of the local people from the area knew that he had been on the Earth for over one hundred and sixty years.

He sat on a chair he had made from oak and white Burch wood and eyed the valley that showed the meandering trail snaking into the distance. As his hounds lay next to him, he patted their heads and rubbed their ears as he said, "I'm sure lucky to have a couple of buddies like you two.

Nobody could ever want more." He had heard all the stories about de Soto and the Indians and how settlers had blazed different paths to the Arkansas valley. He was okay with the stories as long as that was all they were, and nobody interrupted his quiet existence.

One spring day, he was hunting a deer near his cabin when he stumbled upon an intruder on his property. He was at the mouth of the creek where a cave hid a deep crevasse, and water flowed abundantly like a bubble that shot up from the ground. It created a strong stream that began running down the mountain, creating Buttermilk Creek. It had been there for thousands of years.

An unusual-looking man was standing at the bottom of the creek. He entered and exited a cave getting algae and filling a container of fresh water. It wasn't far from Crawford's home, but Crawford got his water from the creek just a little downstream.

Crawford had a gun on the stranger, as he pointed it at his head and growled, "Hey, mister, what are you doing on my property and stealing my water? At first, the alien was startled by the sudden appearance of Crawford and didn't know what to say. He stood there and eyed Crawford up and down while the rifle was pointed at him. He didn't see Crawford as a major threat as he thought, "What a foolish man, using a primitive weapon he thinks might harm me. I could disappear before he could pull the trigger on that gun?" Looking into Crawford's eyes, he decided not to kill him with his Ion weapon.

At first, Crawford thought about shooting the guy for being on his property and taking the water without permission. He said to the intruder, "You know you are trespassing on my land, don't you, and that is my water that you are stealing?" The Nether was easygoing and casually looked at Crawford and said, "I mean you no harm, Sir. I know this is your property, but my people, my ancestors, have been coming to this spring for thousands of years and getting the water and the algae we need."

Crawford was startled as he said, "So, who the hell is your people, and what gives you the right to trespass on my land?" The Nether calmly said, "I'm sorry if I offended you. I'm from the Nethers dimension and on a mission to retrieve the Algae and water to return to my planet. Crawford said, "I got a real doozy here. This guy must think I'm stupid."

He said to the Nether, "Why don't you go get your water somewhere else and leave mine alone?" The Nether said, "We would if we could, but the water and algae here are unique, and there is no other like it in the universe where we can get it."

We make a healing salve from the algae that you can put on a recent wound, and it will heal almost instantly, and the water helps to extend a person's life." Crawford knew his water was pure but was having a tough time with what the alien told him about the salve and prolonging life."

The alien reached into his pocket and pulled out a small metal container with a lump of green salve inside. He cautiously moved closer to Crawford and handed it to him. He said, "Here, you can have this just in an emergency. You rub it on a cut or wound, and it will immediately start to heal."

As Crawford reached out and took the metal container, the alien said, "My name is Krasteem," Crawford reluctantly said, "My name is Crawford Brumley. I've lived up here for years, and I've never seen you or any of your people around here before." Krasteem said, "We are usually more discreet in our harvest and do it at night. I'm sorry if I scared you." Crawford tried to act tough and said, "I'm not scared, just a little angry to catch you here taking the water."

Crawford nervously laughed, saying, "Your entire story seems way out there to me." The Nether told him he would tell him everything if Crawford promised he would not let other humans know what he was doing there.

Crawford jokily went along with Krasteem, thinking the guy must be telling him nothing but a big lie, and said, "Of course, I won't tell anyone. It's on my property. I don't want a whole slew of people coming up here tramping around on my land." Krasteem said, "If they knew the healing powers of this water and the algae, you couldn't keep them away. Thousands, maybe millions, would be trying to get their hands on the precious substance.

Then things got a little more serious, as Krasteem told Crawford about the benefits of the water and algae. He said, "Whoever drinks directly from the spring where the Algae grows will extend their life for hundreds of years. The people on my planet are over one thousand years old from drinking the water and consuming the Algae from this spring." He then showed Crawford the algae they mix with their own compounds and the water together. "Would you like to see the source?" the alien asked Crawford. Crawford, taken back, said, "The Source?" Follow me, Krasteem said as he walked up the hill to the cave's opening. Crawford reluctantly followed behind the alien and then stopped and looked around and, seeing no threat, ducked inside the cave.

The cave was a small opening of fewer than five feet. Once the two had gone into the cave approximately ten feet, the opening widened to where they could stand. Once they got to the end of the cave entrance, it entered into a large room with a fast-flowing stream at its far wall. The stream then flowed under the mountain wall and down the mountain. Crawford could see to the left an entry carved into the wall. He saw Krasteem enter a small room and stood beside a fountain of water flowing out of the ground. It went over the side of the rocks and into the stream. Surrounding the water from the ground was an abundance of algae growing freely. A shard of light beamed down on the fountain from a fissure where the mountain had separated and opened a crevice from the top. It shimmered in the light. "This is the source," Krasteem proudly acclaimed.

He said, "You have heard of the Lost Ark of the Covenant?" Crawford said, "Yes, of course, everyone has heard about it because it's in the Bible." Krasteem said, "You must protect this site like the Ark of the Covenant. Nobody else can ever know its location. He pointed his arms at Crawford and said, "Take a look at yourself. Have you ever noticed that you haven't been aging?" he asked. Crawford took a minute and eyed himself carefully. "Yes, I've never been able to figure that out. Is it because of the water and the algae?" Krasteem said, "Yes, it's been keeping you the same age for years and your dogs too. Have you noticed your dog's living an exceptionally long life?" Crawford replied, "Yeah, I wondered about that. I kept thinking they were going to die on me at any time. I've been worried about losing them."

He told Crawford that the water feeds into the creek that goes past his land, but it loses most of its ability to prolong life as it leaves the source and goes further down the mountain. After talking for a while, Krasteem said, "I know this is a lot for you to understand, but I will be back to harvest more Algae from time to time in the future, and I can answer more questions for you then." Crawford said, "Ok, make sure you come and see me the next time you are here. And you don't have to worry about me pointing a gun at you. I will protect this secret with my life."

They wished each other well as Krasteem reached over with his right hand, passed it over his left wrist, and instantly disappeared. Crawford stood there for an extended time, trying to believe and understand what had just happened. He was talking to Krasteem, and then he disappeared right before his eyes in an instant.

At first, Crawford wondered if he had some illusion, a daydream. He thought about everything and couldn't find a reasonable explanation for what Krasteem had told him. The more Crawford thought about what Krasteem said, the more he realized that he wasn't aging over the years. He was the same age as when he first arrived on the property and built the cabin. He reasoned that what Krasteem told him regarding the water and the algae must be true.

During his years on the mountain, he had met Charlie and Orville, searching up in the hills for an excellent place to get water for their whiskey. He liked them, became friends, and told them to go several miles downstream. He told them they would find an excellent water pool somewhere in Buttermilk Creek, and they could make their Moonshine out of that water. He told them it would be the best Moonshine anyone could ever drink because of the properties in the water. But he told them to make sure they promised never to tell anyone where they got their water, or all the moonshine makers would be fighting to get their water from there. They made a pact with each other to keep the water a secret.

## Chapter 18 - The Hidden Source

The "de Soto" trail was created and mapped to mark the direction Hernando de Soto of Spain and his men had taken exploring the Arkansas valley and where Caddo Gap later sat. Indigenous peoples, called Indians, who occupied this part of the country were very much aware of these outsiders venturing into their homeland and did not like sharing their land with the newcomers.

1541! This region of Arkansas had been easily traveled, but the portion of the high wooded country was dense, dark, and challenging to traverse. The two hundred men forged forward, led by Hernando de Soto and his Lieutenants, urging the men to stay focused on finding fertile lands and gold and riches they would take from the Indians. However, the Indians would have none of it because treaties had been broken and promise not kept, making them wary and suspicious of the Spaniards.

The first arrow cut through the neck of one of de Soto's men, and the man dropped to the ground wrenching in pain as he lay dying. A chorus of high shrieking screams erupted from the surrounding woods as a hundred or more of the battle-thirsty warriors rushed at the Spaniards from the woods. The warriors carried weapons they had used for centuries, axes, the bow and arrow, and slender knives. The Spaniards were equipped with the latest weapons of the European nations. The Snap lock rifle, the precursor to the Flintlock, had just become usable in Spain, and de Soto had his men equipped with this weapon. DeSoto and his officers wore their Flintlock pistols next to their Sabers made from hardened metals. Though not highly reliable but effective, the Flintlock rifles and pistols gave the men an advantage over the weapons the Indians used.

Many of the Indians died in their advance on the Spaniards, but de Soto lost thirty men in the skirmish, which left over two hundred of the Indians dead or dying. Hermando's comrades systematically killed all wounded enemies with their Sabers and long knives. They then moved forward through the thick forest in their pursuit of a village.

Ominous clouds hung overhead and shielded the sunlight from making its way through. A heavy mist blanketed the area, and the daylight still fought to make its presence as morning crept over the mountain peaks. And yet the men still trudged on.

Hermando de Soto and his soldiers had made the walk through most of the previous day and during the night through thick forest and swampy underbrush to make it to this lush mountaintop facing the waterfall. The trek from the village of Casqui had been arduous, but he and his men were at long last approaching their destination for lost Gold and the key to eternal youth.

The conquest of the village had been swift and complete. Taking one of the village elders and their chieftain, he tried to reason and bargain with them for their disclosure of their riches. But one bit of information continually came up. That was the fierce protection of their Devine source. Hermando demanded the location of the la Fuentes de la Eterna Juventud, the fountain of youth, as he had interpreted it.

The chieftain demanded gold be laid before de Soto. Once that was done, de Soto again demanded the location of the source of the fountains. Seeing no concede from the chieftain, de Soto threatened to kill all the villagers and burn the village to the grown. As de Soto rallied his men to begin the massacre, an older woman walked up to de Soto and placed a parchment in his hands with a map drawn from her hand of the location of the water source.

De Soto ceased the activity and called his men to action in preparation to leave the village and ascend the mountain to the drawn location. "Finally, the source and my victory," he thought as Hermando gazed up at the waterfall and a light half-hidden trail meandering up to a cavern on the side of the mountain.

Suddenly a thousand Indians fell upon the conquistadors from the thick forest and began killing the soldiers in masse. Hermando had brought along three Knights on this exploration and tasked them to be his guard.

The soldiers fought bravely but were no match for the onslaught of natives, many from the village of Casqui and many more from the surrounding villages. Seeing that his men were being annihilated, de Soto ordered a retreat, but he could see it was useless. One of the Knights used his body to shield de Soto and was struck dead, but de Soto received a near-fatal blow rendering him useless and leaving the other two knights to protect and retreat with their leader.

Taking five surviving men, the two knights grabbed de Soto and made their way back down the mountain to their ship, and the remaining men moored at the Mississippi River. The Indians roared their victory yells and allowed de Soto and the men to leave, protecting their source and taking back their land.

The Caddo Gap location is where de Soto and his men could go no further west without being forced back to where they had come from by the local Indians.

Many explorers and conquers to the Arkansas valley area over the centuries were turned away or killed, except the people from the dimension of the Nethers. The Nethers had come to the Arkansas region thousands of years before Hermando de Soto.

Surveying and mapping the area, they interacted with the local tribes. Using sophisticated translation devices, they easily communicated with the natives and endeared themselves to the indigenous people, even somewhat protective of them.

But the natives saw these visitors traveling to their villages in flying machines and Devine devices such as the translator and their manor of dress. For that reason, they saw the Nethers as Gods and gladly yielded all of their knowledge and resources to them. Including the source of their precious water and its remarkable abilities.

The people from Nether, in turn, took the waters from the source and turned them into medicines and salves that they used for themselves and the indigenous villagers. Even somewhat protective of them, allowing them to progress in their evolution at their own pace and level. Thus, creating a symbiotic relationship that existed for hundreds of years.

Siratchik (DeSoto) had heard the rumors and stories of the healing waters all of his life as a young child and adult while living on Nether. As he grew older, he became more fixated on the stories. He became an explorer and went on many state-sanctioned explorations in the Nethers galaxy. But his thoughts were always about keeping his mind on his goal of finding la Fuentes Juventud (The Fountain of Youth).

As Siratchik reached adult maturity, he faced the choice of all creatures of the universe who have a choice of free will, and he chose the path of evil and began his life as a criminal.

Chapter 19 – Zak investigates Harley's death

Hearing about the death of Harley, Captain Hiller quickly contacted Zak and said, "Hey Zak, you're not going to believe this, but there was another one of those laser-like killings, but it happened in a small town called Caddo Gap, Arkansas. The guy had a wound in his forehead that resembled a laser weapon wound like the ones that killed the people in Florida. Isn't that town one of the areas you told me you were interested in checking out because of two brothers that make moonshine there? Zak said, "Yes, it is on my list to follow up on because of the recent leads I've been collecting from that area. Who was the guy that was killed?

Hiller said, "The victim was an unassuming fifty-eight-year-old man named Harley Mathews. He and his family have owned a little grocery store in Caddo Gap for years. He was a family guy with two grown children and a wife. The entire family helped out at the store. Everyone from those parts knew and liked Harley and his family.

None of the locals believe something like that would happen in their small town. The locals are up in arms and want to know why Harley was killed. He never went anyplace, just worked the store and was a good family man." Zak said, "Chuck, you and I know there is always a reason something like that happens. It might be someone with a grudge or as simple as someone that owed money to the store. He crossed somebody somehow."

Hiller said, "We are concerned about the weapon used to kill him. The newspaper stated that he was killed with an unusual weapon that looked like one of some unknown origin. Now, all those people are carrying guns and vowing to avenge Harley's death." Zak said, "Yeah, those people are close-knit and look out for each other. I hope they don't start killing each other or the wrong people before I get there."

Hiller told him that Harley's body was at the morgue in Glenwood, Arkansas. He said, "Take a look at his body and see if the wound fits the same method of operation as the people murdered in Florida. It sounds like it was to me." Zak said, "Yes, I will check it out as soon as I get there and let you know what I find."

He told Hiller, "One of my major leads from my footwork in Florida was a couple of brothers named the Carver's, from Caddo Gap. They make illegal Moonshine up in those Ozark mountains and sell it to all the locals. This guy from where the Carver's live turns up dead with a laser hole in his head. This entire puzzle is making a little more sense to me now." Hiller asked, "Is there anything you would like to share with me?" Zak said, "Not, right now, my research is only speculation at this point, but I believe I'm closing in on the purpose of all those deaths. I don't know who's behind it yet, but I think it has something to do with the Fountain of Youth aspect we have been investigating. As soon as I know anything, I will let you know immediately. I'll get out to that area tomorrow." Hiller said, "Ok, calm those people down and let's talk again tomorrow." "You got it, sir," Zak replied.

The next day Zak went to the morgue and talked to the mortician. He pulled back the sheet that covered Harley's body and instantly saw the apparent wound on his forehead. Not a scratch anywhere on his body, just the wound in the middle of his head. As Zak examined the body, he could tell it appeared to be consistent with the same type of weapon used on the victims in Florida. He whispered, "Yes, it's the same or the same type of weapon used in both areas."

Zak called Hiller to let him know it looked like one of the Ion weapons from an alien had killed him. He told Hiller, "The Carver brothers are the two men I need to talk to, but I will have to go to the town and see if I can talk to some of Harley's angry neighbors and friends. What do you think about me spending a couple of days down here in this area?" Hiller replied, "That is a good idea. See if you can get to the root of what is happening there. But don't tell the locals about the aliens possessing a weapon like that. It could cause panic among them. Those people might start shooting helicopters out of the sky." Zak replied, "Ok, I will talk to you again in a few days after I talk to some of them."

When Zak arrived in Caddo Gap, a group of locals was milling around at the store, speculating about what happened to Harley. Zak parked his vehicle about forty yards away from the crowd and slowly made his way to them. The people were angry, and a few were waiving their weapons, saying they would get whoever did that to Harley.

He told the people that he was Zak Thomas and that he was from Homeland Security and sent there on special duty to find out what happened to Harley. He told them that even though the police departments had investigated Harley's death, he was also sent to examine the murder and see if he could find out who killed him.

When the people discovered Zak was from Homeland Security, they asked him many questions. He had to tell them to slow down, that he would try and answer all their questions one at a time. The one question on everyone's mind was what type of weapon killed Harley. People from that area had been around guns their entire lives, and nobody had ever seen a wound like the one on Harley's forehead.

Zak tried to sidestep the issue somewhat as he told them he believed it might have been done with a new weapon recently introduced by a manufacturer. He wasn't going to scare them by telling them it may have been a laser Ion weapon used by aliens from another planet. Zak answered all the questions they asked him during his interviews. He promised them he would find out what happened to Harley and let them know once he had that information.

When he was almost finished talking, he asked if anyone had seen any flying craft that may have landed or crashed near the town the day or the night before Harley was killed. Everyone said they hadn't seen anything.

After the meeting, Zak was approached by a young man in his early twenties. His brown hair was a little long and somewhat fuzzy, and he wore clean overalls over his clothing. Zak could tell the guy was a local from the area by how he was dressed and the way the guy talked. Before talking to Zak, he looked around to ensure nobody could hear him. He sheepishly approached Zak and said, "Mr. Thomas, my name is Franklin Moore. I didn't want anyone else to know it, but I saw a craft fly in and land up the canyon about fifteen miles from here." He pointed to an area that was deeper into the Ozark hills.

He said, "I was coon hunting with my two hounds, and it was about four in the morning when I saw something fly in and land up there. At first, I thought it was a helicopter or something. It flew in fast, but it was weird because it wasn't making a sound. It instantly came to a complete halt about twenty feet off the ground. It hovered briefly, then settled down in the dense woods. It was about five miles from me when it landed, but it was dead silent that night, and you could hear noises for miles. I was getting tired, so I tried to believe it was just a helicopter, so I didn't go check it out. The more I thought about it the next day, the more I realized it wasn't a helicopter because I had never heard any sounds coming from it.

Zak was up close to him by then and listening to his every word as he said, "Hey, Franklin, that is great news. That is what I was hoping to hear from someone from around here. Do you think you have time to take me up to the area and show me where you saw that thing land?" Franklin replied, "Yeah, I could take you up there, but it will take a while to get there and back." Zak said, "That's no problem with me, I'll get what I need, and we can leave." He pulled his car up and parked behind Franklin's pick-up on the side of the dirt road. He jumped inside Franklin's truck and thanked him for taking the time to show him the location.

While they were going up the winding dirt road, Zak phoned Hiller and told him he was following a lead on the murder of Harley and would get back to him the next day.

When they got as far as they could drive, Franklin jumped out of his pickup and walked around to the other side as Zak jumped out. He said, "You will have to take an animal trail from here because this is as far as we can go in a vehicle. He pointed to the northeast and said, "That plane, or whatever it was, landed northeast of here about five to six miles, and it's heavily wooded in that area. It would be a great place to hide something you don't want anybody else to see what you're hiding. What do you think it was, Mr. Thomas?" Zak said, "I don't know, but I hope I can find out." Zak thanked him for bringing him up to the area and pointing him in the right direction. I'll get a fresh start in the morning and come up here and see if I can find where it landed. Who knows, it may still be there."

Charlie told Orville after Harley was killed that they needed to arm themselves and lay low for a while to see what would happen. He told Orville, what if we were the real targets the killer wanted to kill instead of Harley? He said, "Harley was dead right after we delivered our final delivery of moonshine to him. You know, Orville, something strange is happening here, you see daddy, and then Harley gets killed. Maybe it's some omen that we should slow down on making shine for a while, change our ways, or do something different." Orville replied, "I know what you mean. This whole thing here scares the hell out of me. I have the heebie-jeebies right now, Charlie." Charlie said, "Get out a couple of your guns and have them loaded just in case we need em. We'll wait and see if someone comes up here looking for us." If they do, we'll blow the hell out of them," said Orville.

The next day Zak took off from Caddo Gap before noon, and it took him four hours to hike back to where Franklin believed the craft had landed. He fought and dredged his way through thick brush and trees. He was about to give up searching when, much to his surprise, he found the craft perched in the middle of hickory and pine trees near thick brush. It was a little off course from where Franklin thought it had landed, being a little higher up the hills toward Bear Den Hollow.

Zak decided to hide and see if he could see any activity coming from the craft. After watching for several hours, he didn't see anything happening inside or around the craft. Zak decided to get close to it and see what happened. He slowly approached it with his laser weapon drawn and ready in case he needed to fire upon the occupants. Once closer, Zak waited to see if he could hear anything inside but didn't. He tapped on the outside of it, and there was no response.

Zak knew the alien he was pursuing was possibly on a mission to kill a few more locals. But Zak wasn't sure who the alien was after, especially after he had killed Harley for little or no reason. But Zak believed it had something to do with the Carver brothers and their moonshine but wasn't sure. He believed the alien suspected the Carver brothers knew something about what he was looking for and where it was located.

As he left, he entered the ship's coordinates with headquarters and returned to his car. On the way down the canyon, he called Hiller again and told him he had found an alien spacecraft up in the woods of Arkansas and believed it belonged to the rogue alien. He told Hiller he believed it to be a Nether craft but didn't want to disturb it until he knew who the occupants were that flew the craft.

Chapter 20 – Give up or your dead

Charlie and Orville's house was about a half-mile off the old dirt road that headed up the canyon to where Crawford Brumley lived. It was an older two-bedroom house that had been in the family for several generations. It was perched on top of two acres that had been cleared from the middle of the forest. It had a patio facing the canyon and the hills toward the Ozarks. They had a riding mower and kept the weeds and grass on the property mowed short.

Neither of the boys had ever been married, although they had girls who would hang out with them when they were not making their moonshine. Orville liked a girl named Ellawisa and would hang out with her when he could. The other girls would spend time at the house so that they could taste the free Shine.

A lot of the homemade brewed alcohol was so strong in alcohol content that it burned from the time it hit your tongue down into the deepest part of your stomach. That was not the case with Charlie and Orville's brew. It was a little smoother and didn't burn quite as strong on the way down as the others did when a person would take a drink.

It had just gotten dark in the canyon, and the nighttime was so dark and quiet it was like being locked in a dungeon except for the crickets and other insects humming their tunes. It was so dark you could hardly see anything unless it was right before you. That was one reason Charlie and Orville stayed inside most of the time. Like many from those parts, they were a little superstitious because of stories their family members passed down from generation to generation about The Hairy Man. Many believed The Hairy Man lived in these woods and would get you if you stayed out late at night in the hills.

Already on edge from Harley's killing, Charlie and Orville were nervously talking when a deep voice yelled to them from outside. Orville immediately jumped to his feet like he had been slapped and said, "Oh! Shit, Charlie, you were right. Those fuckers are here, and they are after us and our secret." He gripped his rifle tight as DeSoto said, "Hey, you Carver brothers, I want to talk to you, so come outside so we can talk."

Charlie looked over at Orville and said, "See, I told you; they know who we are. We ain't going out there. Get ready; those Son of Bitches is here." Orville replied, "What do you think they want with us, Charlie?" He yelled out, "Our whiskey secrets, what else?" Orville replied, "We ain't given that to nobody. They'll have to kill us first." They sat there, not moving and trying to figure out their next move. Charlie yelled to DeSoto, "Are you with the law enforcement agency?" DeSoto replied, "Nope, nothing like that, just want to talk to you about that whiskey of yours." Charlie said, "See, I told you, Orville."

Charlie and Orville didn't answer him back, so DeSoto said, "Hey, I want to talk to you about that fine whiskey you boys make. Can we talk about that for a minute?" Charlie said, "I know that voice, that sound like the guy we sold those two jugs of whiskey to for two hundred dollars."

He yelled out to DeSoto, "So what's the problem? Don't you like the whiskey we sold you?" Orville said, "This guy is like a bad dream that won't go away?" Charlie replied, "I told you some strange shit was happening around here, and he's one of them." DeSoto tried to schmooze the Carver brothers when he said, "No, I loved that moonshine. I want to find out where you got the water to make the stuff. It's the best I've ever tasted." Charlie hesitated momentarily and said, "Well, thanks, but we don't give up our secrets to nobody, not even the locals." DeSoto kept talking, but Charlie wouldn't give in to his coaxing.

After going back and forth with their conversation for several minutes, DeSoto began to lose his patience. He finally said, "Look, I have your place surrounded with my comrades, and if you don't give me what I want to know, we will come in and take you hostage and torture you until you are forced to give me that information." Orville said, "What information is it that he wants, Charlie? Is it just the water?"

When he said that, Charlie put his extra weapon by the door and gripped his gun tighter. He told Orville, "Ok, this could be it, Orville. It sounds like they are coming in after us." Orville immediately positioned himself by a window with his extra weapon and ammunition. He yelled, "Come and get us, you sons of bitches." DeSoto had his comrades shoot a couple of rounds into the windows with their Ion guns as a warning.

He waited until the smoke cleared as he yelled, "Do you want more of that coming at you?" When Charlie and Orville recovered from the shock of what happened, they took shots through the windows and into the dark of night to let DeSoto know they were armed and would fight back if they didn't have a choice. Orville yelled to them, "Fuck you guys, we ain't telling you shit."

Zak heard the gunshots as he headed back to town and quickly headed in that direction. He wasn't sure what was happening but figured it might be him since DeSoto wasn't anywhere to be found at the craft. Besides, the weapon's sounds differed from a regular hunting rifle or shotgun. Zak thought it might have something to do with him and the local people.

When he got within a quarter of a mile from the house, he jumped out of his car with his laser weapon and threw a couple of rifles over his shoulder. He headed in the direction of the house. When he got near, he heard a man yelling at the people trapped inside. Then he saw the two men positioned on opposite sides of the house that once again fired their Ion weapons through the windows. The Carvers didn't hesitate as they once again returned the fire.

Zak heard DeSoto yell out that he wouldn't put up with any more of their resistance before he and his comrades went in to get them. Charlie yelled, "Come on, assholes, we ain't afraid of you, and we ain't given in to your demands." DeSoto yelled angrily. If I have to, we will burn your house to the ground and force you out." Orville's eyes got big as he looked over at Charlie and said, "These crazy fuckers."

Zak found a hiding position not too far from the house and began to fire in the direction of the two people with DeSoto. The Carvers heard the shots and began firing their weapons toward the front of the woods again. DeSoto's comrades couldn't see Zak but turned their attention away from the Carver brothers and started firing their weapons in what they thought was Zak's direction. Because the night was so dark, Zak could maneuver from one position to another without being seen by DeSoto or the ones with the weapons.

Now, Zak and the Carvers had DeSoto and his men at a somewhat disadvantage. Seeing that someone else had intervened, DeSoto quickly gave up the fight and ordered his comrades to retreat. He knew he wouldn't get what he wanted from the Carvers that night with the resistance. Before leaving, DeSoto yelled to the Carvers, "This isn't over. I'll be back to get what is mine and what I want." Orville yelled back, "Bring it on, you fucking assholes."

Once the shooting stopped and DeSoto and his comrades left, Zak called out to the Carvers. He said, "This is Zak

Thomas from Homeland Security, looks like we scared those guys away, and they left, but they will come after you again. You need to come to town in the morning and talk to me. I can give you a little insight into what they are after." Charlie yelled back, "Thanks, but we know what they want. They want our secrets to making moonshine." Zak yelled, "You are partly right, but they want much more than just the secret." Zak said, "Make sure you find me in the morning so we can talk. For now, you need to find another place to stay for the night. Just in case they come back while you're sleeping and burn your house down."

Zak figured DeSoto wouldn't try and go after the Carver brothers the rest of that night in fear, and they may have more resistance from whoever was helping the locals. He waited around until the Carvers packed up some of their things and drove off before he walked back to his car and headed into town.

Once Zak was gone, Orville asked Charlie, "What the hell is this all about, Charlie? Do you know what is going on with these people?" Charlie scratched his head and said, "I don't have a clue, Orville. I thought it was about our water and moonshine secrets. But, according to that guy Thomas, it might be about more than our whiskey. We better look this guy up in the morning and find out what he has to say. Get your clothes now, and we'll stay at Cousin Scottie's house for a few days."

Orville said, "I hope those guys shooting at us don't come back and burn our house down while we're gone, Charlie." Charlie replied, "Me either, but at least one thing is good. We won't burn up in the damn thing if they burn it down."

It was around midnight when DeSoto and his comrades made their way back to their craft. Not knowing they had landed only a few miles from Crawford Brumley's home, their craft was sitting almost on top of what DeSoto was so desperately searching so hard to find.

Crawford had spotted their craft when they landed and kept a vigil on it for the past few days to ensure they weren't trying to steal his secret. He had his two hounds with him as he waited for DeSoto and his comrades to return that night. When they arrived at their craft and were within range of Crawford's weapons, he began firing at them. DeSoto yelled, "What the hell is with these people around here? All they want to do is fight." He told his comrades to open fire on Brumley's position until they could board their craft and get out of there.

It wasn't long before one of the hounds was hit by one of the Ion beams and went down. Crawford quickly grabbed the can Krasteem had given him that resembled a chewing tobacco can filled with some green salve-like substance. He reached in with two fingers, took a lump, and immediately rubbed it on the wound where his hound had been hit. He took a canteen filled with water and gave him a drink. It only took a few minutes, but the wound began healing instantly. The dog jumped to its feet and, even with a slight limp, began to howl again at the intruders. DeSoto said, unable to see what had just happened, "Let's not waste any more time with this guy and his dogs. Let's get out of here before reinforcements show up again." They immediately departed before Zak or the government military forces could send troops to engage them.

DeSoto didn't realize how close he was to forcing Charlie and Orville to open their doors, walk out, and spill their big secret. He also didn't know that the Fountain of Youth was just at the top of the mountain and so close to his fingertips.

The following morning Zak was interviewing townspeople when Charlie and Orville came casually walking into the building. Charlie walked over and had his two hands in his overall pockets as he said, "Are you Zak Thomas? Zak replied, "Yes, I am." Charlie said, "I'm Charlie Carver, and this is my brother Orville. Zak said, "Yes, I know who you are. I'm the one who helped you last night. Let's go to the corner table where we can have privacy and talk."

As they sat down, Zak asked, "So how did you like the fireworks last night?" Charlie bowed his back and said, "It wasn't very damn funny." Zak replied, "I know, but those guys that came after you will not give up. They will stay after you until you give them what they want, or they kill you." Orville popped off and said, "Hey fuck those guys. I'll get a few of them before they get me." Zak said, "I love your spirit, Orville, but these beings you're dealing with have extra powers. They can cloak themselves and be inside your house; you would never know they were there. Charlie said, "You mean like being invisible?" Zak replied, "Yes, pretty close, like a shadow, and they have weapons that will kill you if the round hits you anyplace on your body."

Charlie said, "Holy crap, who are these guys, and what is it they want from the two of us?" Zak said, "This has to be a secret between the three of us, and nobody else from this town can know. It may mean your life or death." Orville's eyes widened, and he became uneasy. Zak said, "What we are dealing with is not of this Earth. These beings are aliens. They parked their craft further up in the canyon, and I found it yesterday. I was coming back from there when I heard the fighting between you and them."

Charlie said again, "Aliens, what do they want with our Shine and us?" Zak said, "We believe they are tracking the long-believed extension of life, water, chemicals, and algae back to this part of the country. This alien believes the two of you know where it comes from." Charlie said, "We don't know anything about that stuff. We just make moonshine. That's all we've been doing for years." Orville popped off and said, "What about Crawford Brumley? Does he know?" Charlie immediately told him to shut up his trap. Zak looked at Orville and said, "Who is Crawford Brumley?" Charlie interrupted Orville and told him again to keep his mouth shut. Orville wouldn't say anything else after Charlie said that to him.

Zak looked at Charlie and said, "If you are keeping something from me, it might get you in trouble in the future, maybe even killed." Charlie replied, "It ain't nothing. It only means something to Orville and me." Zak could tell that Charlie was hiding something from him, but he didn't know what it was. He also knew Charlie wasn't going to tell him.

Zak asked Charlie and Orville if they wanted to go into hiding for a while so the government could protect them. Charlie said, "Hell no, we can take care of ourselves. If this guy wants our secrets, he'll have to beat it out of us, burn our house down, or kill us." Zak said, "Ok, I gave you fair warning. I'm not sure when these aliens may come back for you, but they will come back, and I can't stop them." Charlie thanked Zak and told him they would stay armed, vigilant, and stick together.

Chapter 21 – Jerimiah

Only a few days after things died down with the Carver brothers, Zak got a call from Hiller. He said, "You're not going to believe this, Zak, but we have another one of those returnees that have surfaced. This one appears puzzling and different from the last ones we keep under lock and key. The local police have asked the military to get involved because this guy has a bizarre story he is telling. We're unsure if he's nuts or just a displaced alien from one of those distant planets. I'd like you to meet with him and let me know your analysis of him after you talk to him."

Zak said, "Can you tell me a little about his story? Is he someone that disappeared from the past and now reappeared, like the others? Hiller replied, "No, this guy is not like the others. We don't know where this guy came from, but he says he is from another dimension. He was captured stealing food from a store in the small town of Mt. Shasta, California. He was dressed and looked like any typical person in his early to mid-thirties. I don't know if he is one of the people you are following up on with the Fountain of Youth or an alien. There's something different about him and the location where he was arrested. It just seems strange to me."

Did he indicate where he came from and why he stole food from the store?" asked Zak. "We've had psychiatrists and military personnel interviewing him for a few weeks, but they can't tell if he is mentally deranged or just made up some crazy story. They say it's hard to tell if he's lying about everything."

Zak asked, "Where is the military keeping him, and when do you want me to go see him?" Hiller replied, "He's down there where we have Truman housed at Area Fifty-One. He claims his name is Jerimiah Johansson. I'd like you to get down to see him tomorrow if you can?" Zak replied, "Ok, I'll get the information on him and head out to meet tomorrow afternoon with him." Hiller said, "That would be great. Just let me know what's going on with him after you talk with him."

The following day when Zak arrived at the base, he was immediately cleared to enter. Once inside, he was escorted to a secluded room where Jerimiah was being kept under guard. He was sitting hand-cuffed to a metal table and didn't seem very happy about being restrained. He seemed a little irritable and frustrated.

Zak went over and slowly pulled up a chair and introduced himself. He told Jerimiah he was sorry they had him hand-cuffed, but it was standard with the military and new detainees. Especially ones that had broken the law. Jerimiah yelled, "Detainee, why am I being called a detainee?" Zak calmly talked to him and got him to relax so he could ask him questions. Zak said, "Once we get things figured out, you will be free to return from where you came. I'm the person that will help make that determination, but first, you have to tell me your story."

Zak softly said, "I want you to know that I'm not like the other military people that have been interviewing you these past few weeks." Zak looked him in the eyes and said, "I deal with people and events not always from this planet." Zak hesitated for several seconds as he studied the man's facial expressions when he said that to him. He said, "When you say people from other planets do you mean interdimensional beings or aliens?" "Yes, exactly like them," replied Zak.

Jerimiah yelled, "Finally, I have someone I can talk to that may try to understand me and what I've been trying to tell those others who have interviewed me. They act like they think I'm crazy." Zak replied, "Well, maybe your story does seem a little crazy to them, but I'm keeping an open mind."

He said, "I've been trying to tell them I'm not from this Earthly dimension. I'm from a parallel dimension. It's much like your three-dimensional planet here on Earth." He hesitated for a moment as he looked Zak in the eyes to see how Zak might react to what he had just said. Do you think I'm crazy, Zak, like the other people that interviewed me?" Zak replied, "So far, no, I've already been to three or four dimensions and planets in my career, so it's not bizarre or far-fetched. You're right. Your situation is a little different. It's why the military sent me here to talk to you."

Zak asked, "So what planet or dimension do you call home? I have friends that are Nethers from another dimension and planet, so I'm aware there are a lot of other planets that have beings on them." Jerimiah smiled and said, "Great, maybe you can help me get back to my dimension and my people. It seems you understand there are other planets and beings, but I'm none of those." Zak thought, "Wait, what?"

It perked up Zak's attention, and he said, "Ok, so if you're none of those, then where exactly are you from." Jerimiah said, "Do you remember seeing stories or reading about ancient cities that have been temporarily seen in the sky by the Earthlings? There have been high-rise buildings and even parts of cities seen from various places all over Earth?" Zak replied, "Yes, I remember reading about some of those sightings being spotted and even seeing pictures taken in China and other countries of those sightings." Jerimiah said, "The people here on Earth try to call those sightings pareidolia, which is just a word for visual hallucinations. I can tell you that when they are seen, they are not hallucinations and are real."

"When people on Earth see those sightings, our parallel dimension somehow collides and connects with the same dimension as Earth. For a brief period, usually twenty to thirty seconds, but sometimes longer, our cities can be seen in your sky, and we can see yours. Still, the visions disappear almost as quickly as they appear, making you wonder how or why that happened."

There are millions of people that live in our parallel dimension, just like all the people here on Earth. We have thousands of cities, streets, electricity, and natural gas, just like you have here. Our people have everyday things we do, just like your people. We believe in God and other religions. Like your dimension, we have hobbies, jobs, sports, everything. Every once in a while, a person from Earth travels through an open portal into our world. The same is similar to our world. I accidentally got caught outside the portal. I came out at Pluto's cave which is underneath Mt. Shasta." Zak interrupted him and said, "Yes, I'm familiar with that cave and that portal."

Jerimiah said, "I was with two other friends that wanted to breach the portal to see what would happen. Once we did, we somehow separated and couldn't find each other. I spent time looking for them with no luck. I began to get hungry, so I went into one of the local stores. I didn't have anything to pay for the food, so I just took what I wanted and began to leave. Your police officers came and arrested me before I could get back to the portal at Pluto's cave. He frowned and said, "That's when I was, as you say, "Detained."

I need your people to release me so I can return to the portal and get back home. I need to get back to my dimension and my friends and life. I don't want to stay in this dimension. I learned a good lesson and realized I don't fit here. Your people are different than ours." Zak was fascinated with his story, but something didn't seem right to him. Zak felt like Jerimiah was partially truthful with him, but he felt he was still hiding something and didn't know what it was. Before he was through interviewing him, he was going to find the underlying cause of his concern.

He told Jerimiah they needed to take a break for about a half hour. He told him to relax until he went to the bathroom, grabbed a cold drink, and talked to his superiors. He had the guards bring over a couple of cold bottled waters for Jerimiah and let him go to the bathroom while he was out.

Zak needed some time to think about this guy's story and collect himself before he went back to confront him again. What happened to his friends? How could they become separated when they came together? He wondered why this guy would travel without money or payment value. He had to have been told about our monetary system by some of his friends that had been to our dimension before. He knew he couldn't just walk into a store and walk out without being caught or punished for trying to steal. He also wondered why this guy didn't have any ID or anything to prove who he was and that what he was saying was true. Before talking to him again, he wanted to formulate a different approach with Jerimiah and see if that would get him to open up more.

When Zak returned to talk to Jerimiah, he was a little sterner in his approach as he sat across from him. Zak said, "Ok, Jerimiah, I've been thinking about everything you've told me so far, and to be honest with you, some things aren't adding up for me. You say you were with some other friends, yet your friends are nowhere to be found. How is that possible when you come together? You have no form of currency to pay for something you stole, no ID. There is nothing that proves your story to me is real.

Jerimiah looked startled as he stared at Zak. He thought Zak believed everything he had told him. There was an awkward moment as the two just sat and stared at each other.

After a few minutes, Jerimiah realized that he couldn't fool Zak any longer and finally broke the silence. He said, "You're right, Zak. There are a few things I've kept from you. Almost everything I've told you about my dimension, our people, is true. The only thing I kept from you is that I'm not a time traveler, I'm an interdimensional traveler representing several dimensions, and I came by myself. I didn't come with two others, as I said earlier."

Zak said, "So why not tell me that in the beginning? Why lie about it? You said you came through a portal; don't you think that sounds bizarre for most people here on Earth?" Jerimiah replied, "You are right, but that's how I got the attention I needed."

Zak said, "Start again and tell me the real truth about what you are doing here. Were you sent here to observe our dimension at the request of your government or military?" Jerimiah's attitude changed and softened as he replied, "Yes, I came as a representative at direct orders and consent of the Heads of State of our dimensions. My orders are to determine how much Earth has progressed in military power.

We have been keeping an eye on Earth for several thousand years. But only recently have we been concerned about the wars, threats of wars, and the nuclear explosions on Earth and in space by the different governments of Earth. Earth's knowledge of nuclear power and energy-directed weapons has increased dramatically over the past hundred years. We desire to make sure the war-like attitude possessed by Earthlings is not a threat to our dimension and others in the Universe.

I've been on Earth for a few months now, observing different countries' military and nuclear sites. During my stay, I reported my findings regarding your nuclear and energy-directed weapon growth to my superiors.

It was not an accident that I was captured. I allowed it to happen on purpose. I knew that once I was captive and told law enforcement the same story, I told you they would turn me over to your military for questioning. It worked, and they confined me to the most secure military base in the United States, Area Fifty-One. That gave me a perfect chance to observe the inside workings of your military, and I was also able to get a lot of information."

Zak was surprised by what Jerimiah was telling him as he replied, "I never expected you to tell me something like that. After all your research, do you feel like you got the answers to the questions you were searching to find? Do you think we are a threat to your dimension?" "I've learned immensely since I've been here. Earthlings have advanced greatly over the past one hundred years, but I don't think military sophistication is capable of an interdimensional war with us. I don't think they want a war with us either."

Our weapons are far superior to the still developing and primitive weapons you have here on Earth. Earth's military would be no match for ours or the other dimensional weapons. Besides, your society has enough domestic issues to deal with rather than concern themselves with other dimensional beings."

He said, "Our people are no threat to the people on Earth. We are a peace-loving race, and we don't possess the desire to destroy another civilization just because we can. The ones in my dimension live in harmony with each other."

Zak spent a few more hours with him before Jerimiah asked if he might be able to help get him back to the portal so he could return home. Zak was somewhat perplexed by everything he and Jerimiah talked about but felt comfortable that Jerimiah was being honest with him. He said, "Let me try and clear everything with my superiors, and we'll see if we can get you to the portal soon." Jerimiah thanked him.

Zak called Hiller and explained everything he and Jerimiah discussed during their conversation. He told Hiller that Jerimiah was from a parallel dimension almost intertwined with Earth's dimension, and he was an interdimensional traveler that had traveled to Earth's dimension to observe us.

The captain asked, "What do you think we should do with him? Is it safe to let him go?" Zak replied, "Yes, Sir, I know he's no threat to us. He wants to get back to his dimension. We need to give him a military escort back to Mt. Shasta and turn him loose at the base of the caves, where he says he can enter a portal inside the caves that will take him back to his dimension. Hiller said, "Ok, we will take him back tomorrow.

Chapter 22 - The Right Position

The night was extremely dark, but the man walked briskly and remarkably fast, given the low visibility. His pursuer stumbled along the path, hesitant in his pursuit but still keeping pace with his mark. At the end of the street's alley, the trail abruptly stopped. The pursued man turned to face his follower and then yelled out, "You can stop there," but the figure continued to come closer until they were within mere yards of each other. "Are you so determined that you would kill me?" The man asked his pursuer.

The figure stepped a little closer, and the distant light of a lamppost shone slightly on Desoto's face. "I would kill anyone who would rob me of what is mine," DeSoto responded. And then added, "Let me ask you, do you honestly think you can come to this planet and seek out the algae and not be detected? I've heard of you, coming from the far side of Nether, and your part Human, but your just another thief trying to squeeze in where he's not supposed to be."

"And what are you?" The man asked, "Coming to this planet to plunder its natural resources for yourself. You're no different." DeSoto said, "I hear you've traveled to the galaxy's far reaches, and you've seen things others only whisper about, but have you seen him?" "Who?" The man asked, "Man," DeSoto said, a little irritated in not being understood." "Oh, you mean God," the man said and slightly chuckled, enjoying the frustration he was causing DeSoto.

"Yes, God, Man, whatever the Humans are now calling him," DeSoto said with a slight wave of his hand, "You know you Humans want to be so much like Man, uh, God, but you can only be humankind, you will never have that power."

"No, I've never seen "Him," "I've been close to what I thought was his realm, but it wasn't. As you said, I'm only half Human. I don't want Power or Devine intervention, just riches, Gold, like you. Maybe we can partner up on this venture?" The alien replied and then shifted as he reached into his coat pocket to retrieve a cigarette pack which he showed to DeSoto. "Not interested. Besides, I have all the help I need for now. It would be best if you had come to me in the beginning, I would have hired you, and it would have gone a lot easier on you. By the way, can you shift your position slightly to the right?" DeSoto said. "Why?" the man asked as he lit a cigarette and slightly turned to the right.

"For this," DeSoto said and just as quickly slid a stiletto knife into his right hand and threw it underhanded at the man, which caught him in the right eye, plunging deep into the man's brain. As the man dropped to the ground, DeSoto walked over and hovered over him. One of DeSoto's accomplices emerged from the shadows and stood next to DeSoto, watching the man die.

"That pain in the ass Human, Zak Thomas, is starting to figure some things out," the henchmen said as he looked down. "I'm starting to feel the same way. Let's visit him very soon. DeSoto said, looking up at him." The accomplice just nodded yes.

Zak drove his rental out of the Redding Avis parking lot, pulled to a side street, punched in coordinates for a local chain hotel, and called Captain Hiller.

"Chuck, can you meet me at Mt Shasta with the prisoner Jerimiah? Hiller responded, "Let me finish today, and I'll meet up with you there tomorrow afternoon with the prisoner and another agent." "Looking forward to seeing you," Zak responded.

On the northern side of the California central coast sits a resort hotel comprised of twenty-eight individual rooms in two stories, fourteen on each row. The newer hotel had partitions between each room, providing the guests with a substantial degree of privacy. Open only to the front, which stretched two hundred feet to the sandy beach and the Pacific Ocean. A five-foot dirt bank dropped off to the sand at the end of the hotel's grassy front. The bank ran the length of the hotel.

The shooter checked his watch for the time, finding the evening fading light gave him just enough illumination to see the last top-five rooms situated to his left and plenty of time before total darkness blanketed the building.

Pressed hard against the bank and facing the hotel, he lowered himself to his haunches and reached into his right coat pocket. Taking out the small tactical 4 X 32 sniper scope and affixed it to his Bushmaster AR-15 minimalist rifle. Reaching further into his coat pocket, he removed a silencing suppressor and fixed it to the rifle.

Then rising back to the ridge, he scanned the building through the scope and waited patiently for any occupants to emerge through the slider door to the veranda. Specifically, room two hundred and twenty-eight, the top floor he had covertly, from the beach, watched over the last two days to see how often the man inside stepped out.

Agent Ron Folley with Homeland Security and his wife were vacationing at the resort for a three-night trip. He would be leaving early to catch a flight to Redding, California, to rendezvous with a member of Homeland security and then meet with Zak to escort prisoner Jerimiah to a facility in the Mt. Shasta area.

Hoping to catch a last glimpse of the setting sun and the dark orange hues over the ocean waves while his wife slept inside the room, agent Folley stepped out onto the balcony and looked out at the rolling waves as they glistened in the sun. He took a drink of the Pinot Grigio wine from his glass.

The bullet struck his left temple and passed through his head but threw his body so violently against the partition divider to the other room that it caused the guest of the next room to run out onto her balcony, confused by the loud commotion, not knowing a person had just been murdered in the room next to her.

The shooter aimed at the female's chest as she tried to peer around the railing and the partition. The bullet pierced her heart, killing her instantly. The shooter then attempted to make the shooting look as random as possible, leaving markings of his presence, and then made his way down the beach to his parked car and off toward the highway on his way to Redding, California.

Zak was up early the following day, and after a quick but relaxed workout in the hotel's gym, he exited his room and started toward the hotel's restaurant. Reaching for his cell phone, he called Captain Hiller. "Morning, Captain. Just checking in. Any idea on your ETA?" Zak asked.

"Morning Zak, I should be at the Army National Guard base around noon, and the prisoner Jerimiah will be delivered to us. Just look for the company helicopter. Oh, and also, an agent from Homeland Security named Ron Folley will be helping us with the escort and arriving at your location about the same time I get there." Hiller responded.

"Yes, he just called my hotel room about thirty minutes ago and said he's on his way and should meet me for breakfast at the hotel," Zak said. But it wasn't agent Folly on the phone; it was DeSoto pretending to be Folly.

Chapter 23 - Zak Meets DeSoto

The car sped down highway Interstate 5 on its way to Redding. "It's done, Siratchik. The agent is dead. I also killed the person in the room next to the agent, a female," the driver said. "Did you use the AR-15?" DeSoto asked. "Yes, and I also used the suppressor you gave me. They both worked perfectly," the driver answered.

"We can give thanks to dead Herb in Florida for those items. Ok, meet me in Redding, Roalm, and I should be there in approximately an hour and a half. We got a little behind schedule, but we found the Nether trying to intrude in my business in San Francisco, and I left a blade deep inside his right eye. He won't be stealing from anyone anymore," DeSoto said.

"I'll meet up with the other agent, Zak Thomas, at his hotel, you and Roalm stand by for my word, and once we've killed Thomas, we'll wait for the prisoner Jeremiah and take him back to my ship. He should know where the Algae is located. He better, with what I have planned to do to him. "Yes, I know the plan," the driver replied. "Just do it, DeSoto growled," a slight irritation in his voice.

The Silver Chevy Malibu drove into the hotel parking lot, which was half empty. Pulling into a stall, the driver stopped the vehicle, shut off the engine, and reached for his disposable cell phone. "I'm at the hotel," the driver said. "Good, we'll be there in about a half hour. Get eyes on Thomas," DeSoto said, and don't let him make you. He's pretty sharp, I've heard," he added.

Desoto's henchman exited the car, walked through the courtyard toward the lobby, and then sat on a cushioned chair facing the hotel's restaurant. He saw Zak Thomas walk from the lobby toward the restaurant within twenty minutes, just as DeSoto had told him he would. The henchman texted DeSoto that Thomas was heading to the restaurant as he continued to keep his eyes on him. Within minutes DeSoto arrived at the hotel with his second henchman, Roalm.

While sitting in the passenger seat, he looked down. He passed his right hand over his left wrist, which held the imaginator device, and bringing up the image of Ron Folley, Homeland Security agent, a small void momentarily filled the vehicle, and an odd transformation ensued. Desoto emerged from the vehicle as Agent Ron Folley.

The corridor past the courtyard ran directly into the pool area, which had the hotel's restaurant to its right. DeSoto walked through the Corridor as Ron Folley. He glanced to his left and saw that Roalm had joined his comrade and the two of them briefly glanced back at DeSoto and then quickly engaged in a conversation between them, looking as inconspicuous as possible.

DeSoto, for his part, arched his back and took a casual stance as he opened the door to the restaurant, then panned out over the patrons. Seeing Zak Thomas from the photographs he had brought up on the Internet, he proceeded toward Zak's table.

"Zak Thomas?" The stranger asked. "Yes, are you agent Folley?" Zak asked, looking up at the man from his seat. "I am," the agent answered back. "Have a seat, agent," Zak said, motioning to an empty seat in front of him.

"I have some important papers I need to go over with you in private before your prisoner and his escort arrives," the agent said earnestly, looking down at Zak. Looking up at the man, Zak could see the agent was very intent and looked like a nice enough guy, a sincere type.

"Alright," Zak said, glancing down at his watch and checking the time. Captain Hiller had told him that he should arrive in Redding around noon. Zak had a little more than an hour before that. Standing up, he waived at the server, pointed to his watch, and then tossed a twenty-dollar bill down on the table.

"Follow me. We can go back to my room here at the hotel. You have the papers in your briefcase?" Zak said, glancing down at the case in the agent's left hand. "I do, and also an authorization I need you to sign," agent Folley said.

Zak thought this was odd since the agency had set up the meeting with Jeremiah, and Captain Hiller requested everything Zak had been authorized to do. "Are you familiar with the other Homeland Security agent transporting the prisoner this afternoon?" Zak asked as they walked down the corridor towards Zak's room. "Nope, I never met him, but I'm sure he's proficient. The government trains our people well," the agent answered.

I'm based out of our Seattle office. How about you?" Zak asked as he motioned to the front door of his room and moved his key over the lock sensor. "Oh, I'm what you might call a roving agent. I work out of many different stations. Wherever they need me, I go," Agent Folley said, stepping into the room and ensuring he did not completely shut the door.

"I get that. I do a lot of traveling with the outfit as well," Zak said, reaching for bottled water on the room's table. "Want water?" Zak asked. "No thanks," DeSoto said as he walked toward the bed to place his briefcase on the cover.

At that moment, Zak's cell phone beeped and taking his phone from his sports coat pocket, he read the text in bold letters: ZAK, AGENT FOLLEY FOUND DEAD THIS MORNING, ABORT MISSION IMMEDIATELY. CAPTAIN CHUCK HILLER.

As Zak read the message, agent Folley laid the briefcase on the bed, opened it up, reached in, grasped the Ion pistol inside, and brought it out. Zak's mind was on hyperdrive once having read Chuck's message, and his Taekwondo training took over.

Seeing the pistol lifted from the top of the briefcase and recognizing the type of pistol in the agent's hand, Zak in one leap took a flying jump and then pressed out his right leg at the same time and landed a perfect blow to the agent's right hand knocking the ion pistol away.

Within seconds the front door to Zak's room burst open, and DeSoto's two henchmen ran in and surrounded Zak as DeSoto regained himself and joined the surrounding of Zak. Zak eyed the three aggressors and instantly switched his mind to another time and another advanced training he had undergone.

While Zak was stationed in Subic Bay, Philippines, for three months with the US Marine Corps, he trained alternately with a squad of Filipino Marines who were highly trained in the art of Krav Maga. This hand-to-hand combat method employs the techniques of many different styles.

Their idea of fun was to put four aggressors in a ten-by-ten room with one person in each corner and with you in the middle of the room. Each opponent would use an individual style, boxing, karate, taekwondo, or kickboxing, and you would have to fight off each aggressor until victorious.

In that tight space, the fighting could become intense and sometimes painful. In the three months Zak trained with the Filipino Marines, he got proficient with their methods, particularly the tiny room combat.

DeSoto was the first to advance towards Zak, and Zak wasted no time in advancing back, bringing down a crushing blow on DeSoto's nose and facial area. When DeSoto received the blow, it slammed him hard against the wall and caused him to drop to his knees; shaking his head and his arms willing himself to stay awake, he rose, and as he did, the transformation from Agent Folley fully dissolved and standing before Zak was DeSoto in his true form.

"What the hell are you?" Zak said to DeSoto as he executed a tight jump kick at the advancing aggressor to his right and followed through with a twist of his knees to come face to face with the third aggressor Roalm, who stood ready to plow a bone-crushing blow to Zak's neck. Roalm merely threw up his arms and waived them in retreat. He then ran toward the room's front door and, before running out, grabbed his comrade, and they both exited, leaving Zak standing at the ready and looking down at DeSoto, who had slumped down to a sitting position.

"Let me guess," Zak said, "You're the piece of shit rogue alien who's been tearing up things here on Earth and killing a whole lot of people," as he walked over and picked up the Ion pistol and walked back over to face DeSoto. "Why?" Zak asked. "What is it about this time, power, money? Yeah, probably money, or maybe you're just a crazy lunatic and don't like Earthlings, a lot of that going around."

DeSoto just sat silently and slowly wiped away the blood from his nose and mouth. Then he spoke, "You can call me DeSoto," and spat blood onto the carpet. "I owe you one, big time," he said as he made his way to his feet.

Zak motioned DeSoto towards the door. "You'll get a chance to tell it to my Captain. He'll be in Redding shortly. Right now, we're going to ride to the Army reserve base. You first!" Zak said as he motioned DeSoto out of the room.

As they exited the door, Roalm, standing outside the door and in shadow effect, waited till DeSoto left and then went to hit Zak on the side of Zak's head. Zak saw a shadowy figure as he passed the door, saw DeSoto's reaction to the moment, and ducked back into the room. At that moment, DeSoto went into shadow effect himself, and both he and Roalm fled down the corridor to their comrade waiting in their parked car. Jumping in, they both slammed their car doors as the vehicle sped into traffic and was out of sight.

Zak opened his room door slightly and could see no one in the hall or out front. He then shut the door, walked over to the room's table, picked up a bottle of water and his cell

phone, and, sitting down on a chair, proceeded to call
Captain Hiller.

Chapter 24 – Truman Disappears

It was early in the morning and still cold outside when Zak
got a call from Hiller. Zak put his coffee down and said,
hey Chuck, what up? Pretty early to be calling me, huh."
Hiller said, "The darndest thing has just happened. You
know that kid Truman Wallace? He's disappeared from
our protection. The soldiers have searched the entire place
at the Area 51 facility, and he is nowhere to be found. It
looks like he's missing again."

Zak said, "What, how could something like that happen?
How is that even possible? I thought we had guards that
were keeping an eye on him?" Hiller replied, "We did.
The soldier watching him said he had just disappeared
sometime during the night. The soldier said, "One minute,
he was there, and the next minute, he was gone. It was as if
he vanished into thin air." Zak said, "I can't believe it.
There is something weird going on there?"

After he hung up the phone, Zak was frustrated as he sat on
the porch and sipped his coffee while pondering his
thoughts. Then he started to recreate his last meeting with
Truman to find out if he missed something. After thinking
about things, it hit him right between the eyes. Truman's
parents would not keep him because they said he was not
their son. Everyone believed the parents were just
paranoid, but maybe they were right. Maybe he wasn't
their son. A mother, especially, would know if it were her
son or not.

Zak continued to search his memory regarding their
meeting to see if there was anything else that he may have

missed. Then he said, "Wait a minute. Truman said the people holding him would not take him back, no matter how much he pleaded with them. Then after twenty-five years, they suddenly decide to give in to his wishes of being back home. That seems a little strange. Then a bizarre thought crossed Zak's mind. Wait, what if this kid wasn't who he said he was? What if he were just another one of DeSoto's henchmen and could cloak himself and disappear."

He immediately called Hiller back and explained everything he had been thinking about during his last meeting with Truman. He said, "What if that kid weren't a kid but one of DeSoto's henchmen that had shape-shifted from an adult to a kid so that he could find out information for DeSoto? That DeSoto is clever, and I wouldn't put it past him.

Hiller said, "Do you know how crazy that sounds, Zak?" Zak replied, "Yes, it's crazy, I know, but think about it for a minute. His parents wouldn't take him back because they said he wasn't their son. He's held captive and grilled by the military and disappears into thin air. Only an alien would have the ability to disappear like that." Hiller said, "You're right, that would explain him disappearing, but if he was DeSoto's man, he sure had all of us fooled."

Zak said, "Yes, but remember the Nethers have all those abilities we just talked about and more. They can even cloak themselves, hiding and walking out of prison without being seen." Hiller said, "If that is the case, how do we find this kid or guy now?" Zak replied, "We can't, his mission is over for DeSoto, and we'll never see him again. I've gotta find DeSoto and his two accomplices and try to stop them from this crazy quest they're on. That may be a little harder task after my recent encounter with him. He's like a chameleon that can change into anything he wants at a moment's notice. He is fully aware that I'm after him now."

DeSoto had Truman transferred back to his ship in the night. He believed it was time for them to have an important meeting before going further with the Truman charade. Once on board, Truman's image transformed back to a Nether in his original form in his mid-thirties and no longer the young boy he was pretending to be. He quickly said, "Much better! It feels good not to be that kid anymore and return to my true form." The two of them began to discuss everything he had learned while pretending to be the captive nine-year-old missing boy from the past.

He began to tell DeSoto all the details of what he had found out from his captors. He stated the soldiers didn't know about the water and algae or its abilities. But he told DeSoto that one soldier named Zak Thomas had learned much and shared it with me during his visit. He told me the Nethers would never give up their secret about the water and algae to anyone, but you were trying to acquire that knowledge for yourself.

"The biggest problem for you, Siratchik, is not finding the formula or its location. It's now the soldier known as Zak Thomas that is hunting you. He's a warrior and is aware of you and your exploits. He's also aware of all the people you have killed and encountered in searching for your goal of finding the water and algae. He told me that he would kill you as soon as he got a chance so that you won't kill any more innocent people.

He knows about the water and the algae, but I don't believe he knows where it's located. He seems very good at what he does and may be a significant obstacle for you to overcome. How do we get paid for our time and sacrifices if he kills you, Siratchik?"

DeSoto growled, "That's nonsense; you work for me! I've paid you half of your gold, and you'll get the other half when I get my hands on the source of what I've come here to obtain. I've had confrontations with Zak Thomas, but he doesn't worry me; he just strengthens my resolve. DeSoto looked at his accomplice, who now seemed a bit more assured, and said, "He's clever, but he'll end up just like the others, giving me what I want or dying.

Chapter 25 – Zak Visits Crawford

It had been over a week since Zak had his encounter with DeSoto and his accomplices, and he was starting to wonder where he should go next. Something that kept crossing his mind was what Orville Carver said during Zak's meeting with him and Charlie. Orville had mentioned the name of Crawford Brumley but froze when Zak quizzed him about Crawford. Zak, having the investigative mentality, that name kept haunting him since it was uttered from Orville's lips.

Zak called Hiller and told him he was going to the Ozark Mountains of Arkansas to see if he could hunt down that guy Crawford Brumley. Zak said, "I don't know if he is relevant to DeSoto or the life extension substance, but Orville Carver mentioned his name when I last interviewed him and his brother. Then, when I asked him who Crawford was, his brother Charlie quickly shut him up, not wanting me to know anything about the guy.

I discovered he has lived in the Ozark Mountains about twenty miles up the hills from Caddo Gap. But there aren't many records on him, hardly any at all. It doesn't show a road to his house, so it has to be at the end of one of those dirt roads. It looks like the end of the DeSoto trail. I couldn't even find out how long he's been there, but it appears a while." Hiller replied, "Well, it doesn't seem like much of a lead, but at least you have someone to check. Good luck down there and call me if you need me."

It was mid-afternoon when Zak arrived at his destination. The sun dropped above the trees, and the air was brisk and cold. Before going to Caddo Gap, he got a strong cup of coffee from a local restaurant in Glenwood, not far away. Zak had on the warm clothing that he wore in the Pacific Northwest, so he was comfortable. The air from his mouth burst like a fog when he blew a deep breath after sipping the coffee. He then pulled out his GPS and followed the dirt road that pointed to his destination.

As he went up the road, he said, "Hey, I know this road. I've been on it a couple of times before. The last time I was here, I checked out the Nether craft parked in the woods. It was the night DeSoto and his accomplices' fired shots at the Carvers. It ends about fifteen to twenty miles up there, and then you must walk several miles along the DeSoto dirt trail the rest of the way to Brumley's place. Why would anyone want to live that far away from civilization? Too far to even have to replenish supplies."

All the roads above Caddo Gap that led to the deep forest and high country were rugged, pockmarked, and dirt lined. He sometimes hit the potholes he couldn't see. Occasionally a deer going to its favorite place to eat would shoot across the road in front of him. The birds and animals were coming alive, all searching for food and water. There were few places where the limbs of the trees from one side of the road met up with the ones on the other.

It reminded Zak of roads he'd been on where you had to travel through a tunnel to get to your destination.

As the road traversed higher into the forest, the old road showed signs of some use but very little. Most people who traveled into the mountains above the towns in that area tended to stay off of these roads, particularly this old road, as it was rumored to be dangerous because of the occasional Still that dotted the area but also haunted and the home of wild animals.

Zak pulled his car forward as far as possible up the mountain, looking out the front of his window towards the sky. He could see that it was starting to become nighttime, he wasn't happy about having to travel this road in the darkness of night, but he had one last part of his mission in this part of the country.

He would go to Brumley's cabin and find out what he knew about the secret to the healing powers of those lost waters. Nearing the end of the drivable road, Zak pulled his car to the far side of a small clearing and parked the rental.

Night had overtaken the day, and Zak was fully engulfed in the darkness as he exited the vehicle. He knew he had roughly four to five miles before reaching Brumley's cabin. But Zak had been in many situations evolving darkness and danger. He had his night vision and flashlights to help guide him.

In Afghanistan, trailing the madman Shief, he hid in the darkness of the desert caves that dotted the barren landscape and in the wilds of the Pacific Northwest when he hunted a monster of unimaginable horror.

It took Zak about an hour and a half to get to the end of the road before he jumped out of his rented car and holstered his Ion gun. He also carried an automatic rifle that fit comfortably over his shoulder. He grabbed two water bottles and threw them in the backpack strapped on his back. He also grabbed a couple of packs of beef jerky to have something that would stifle his hunger.

Once he felt ready, he began his trek up the mountains toward the home of Crawford Brumley. Zak could tell that the animals used the trail more than humans. The road had ended in a drivable width and then narrowed to a walkable path Zak now took. The first part of the narrows was extremely dark. The trees grew over each other and formed a tunnel with the floor of the path like cobblestone and uneven to walk with a tiny breeze through the tunneled way.

Halfway through the thick, Zak heard a woman's ear-piercing scream in extreme fear and pain. Then louder, it echoed around the surrounding trees, then died to dead silence, then again as it pierced the night.

Zak could see an opening in the canopy as the trees slightly opened to the thick forest. As he continued on the path, he heard footsteps as they trailed his steps to his right, then stopped when he did. Then they started up again as he continued. Then a shadowy figure appeared to his left and leaned against a huge tree. The figure raked its hand against it, and Zak could hear bark tearing as the tree raked. Walking near the tree, Zak could see four deep-defined claw marks high up on the tree.

Then rounding a bend, Zak could hear heavy breathing. As he stepped into the bend, he saw to his left on the west side of the path. A large black Panther sat on a slight slope, its red radiating eyes glowing in the slight moonlight being exposed. Its large front paws slowly extracted and retracted, showing the huge claws. Very rare and hardly ever seen in these parts of Arkansas, the animal existed in its secrecy, only being talked about in tall tales and legends.

Zak immediately pulled the Ion pistol from his holster as the animals piercing gaze caught Zak, and he matched the animal, staring eye to eye. Sitting dead still, the Panther did not move a muscle other than its black tail that moved periodically back and forth. The tip seemed to shimmer and then rattle like the tail of a rattlesnake.

Zak placed his pistol in his waist holster, raised his arms to full length above his head, and started to curse the animal as loud as he could. "Get the hell out of here, go, get," Zak yelled as he continued to walk to the far right of the path and far from the animal. The Panther only looked at Zak as it stayed mobile and seemed disinterested as Zak walked out of its path and sight.

When finally reaching a reasonable distance from danger, Zak once again pulled the pistol from the holster and proceeded up the path to Brumley's cabin.

When he got close to Crawford's place, he started seeing homemade signs that warned him to stay out, that it was private property. The signs said trespassers would be shot. A chill ran up Zak's spine for a short minute, wondering if this guy might try to kill him. Zak had been in many dangerous situations and believed he could manage this one if he had to use force.

When Zak started getting close to the house, he heard the hound dogs' barks warning Crawford that someone was nearby. Not knowing how many dogs he had, Zak proceeded very slowly and carefully as he got closer. When he got within forty yards of the old house, the dogs ran toward Zak as if they were going to attack him. It made him feel as if they were ready to bite him at any moment showing their canines. They were growling, barking, and snapping at Zak as he moved slowly toward the house. As he got closer, Crawford emerged from the house with a rifle. He yelled, "Hold it right there, or I'll free up my dogs on you, and they will tear you apart. Zak said, "Ok, I'm not moving any further until you tell me I can." Crawford said, "What the hell are you doing on my property, especially after dark?"

Zak said, "Hey Crawford, I'm Zak Thomas, and I'm with Homeland Security. I want to talk to you about an incident nearly a month ago in these woods. Can we take a few minutes and talk?" Crawford thought, "Oh damn, I'm in trouble now." He took a defensive position and said, "Hey, those guys I shot at had no business being on my property. They're just lucky I didn't kill a couple of them." Zak didn't know anything about that encounter but pretended that was why he was there and said, "Yes, the government wanted me to come out and talk to you about what happened. Can you call your dogs off so we can talk for a few minutes? I have guns too, but I don't want to use them, and I especially don't want to shoot a dog."

When he said something about shooting his dogs, it irritated Crawford, and he yelled out. "Yeah, those guys from that helicopter or whatever it was shot one of my dogs here when they tried to shoot me." Zak said, "I have no intentions of shooting anything. I keep the guns for defensive purposes because I don't want to get killed by someone from here. I also don't want to get bit when I don't need to. I want to talk to you about some things. Can we do that, Sir?" Seeing that Zak was sincere, he called his dogs off, and they went and stood by Crawford's side. Crawford patted the dogs on the head to let them know everything was ok. He had a porch with a couple of worn-down hand-made chairs and motioned for Zak to come and sit at one of them.

Once comfortable, Zak introduced himself and shook hands with Crawford. He showed him his Homeland Security badge before sitting down. Crawford had a nasty look in his eyes while studying Zak's face. He wasn't sure if Zak would try and arrest him for shooting at the guys or what was on his mind. He slowly said, "So, am I in trouble with the law?" Zak said, "You don't have a problem with me, but can you tell me what happened?" Zak was fishing to see what Crawford was talking about because he knew nothing about shooting at anyone.

Crawford began to talk slowly about the craft parked not too far away and near his property. He said, "I watched that helicopter or whatever it was for three days. It was parked there when the three men got close to it around midnight on the third day. I was irritated that someone had left it in the forest near my property. I took some shots in their direction to try and scare them away. They shot back in my direction, and damn, guys hit one of my dogs. I thought it killed him, but it was able to survive." Zak looked down at the dog, which had no mark on its body. Zak said, "Where did the bullet hit him? It doesn't look like he had a wound or a scar?"

Crawford quickly realized he had given Zak too much information and said, "Oh, it just glanced off his hip, but he healed up quickly." Zak leaned in toward the dog and said, "That is amazing. It doesn't look like his body has ever been hit by a bullet or anything. What happened to that helicopter or whatever you saw?" Crawford said, "It was the darndest thing, those men got in, and it zipped off so fast you couldn't even follow it through the air in these woods."

Zak's mind was starting to put two and two together. He knew that night must have been the night he ran DeSoto away from the Carver Brothers' house, and they went back and boarded their ship. He also knew that if a person or animal were shot with the Ion gun, it would not survive. "So how did this dog survive the wound it received? Crawford had to have the life-saving salves he rubbed on his dog's wound?" Zak now believed that Crawford Brumley was the one Earthly person that held the secret about the water and algae. How else could his dog heal from an Ion shot and not even have a scar or wound? If the dog had been shot with a regular bullet, he would still have a scabbed over and healing wound.

Zak felt this was the perfect opportunity to share information about the rogue alien with Crawford. He said, "You know, Mr. Brumley, my mission with Homeland Security is to hunt for rogue aliens." Crawford leaned back and said, "What do you mean, rogue aliens?" Zak said, "A rogue alien is an alien that has gone against his planet's orders and demands and trying to enrich himself and gain personal power and wealth. Crawford thought, "This alien stuff is getting too close to me; it's now the second time I've heard about them."

Zak said, "The one I'm hunting is the rogue alien that has been hunting for the formula that gives people the extension of life. He believes the substance comes from somewhere in this area. He and two henchmen killed people in Florida, California, and Arkansas looking for the stuff. He is the one that killed Harley here in Caddo Gap." Crawford's eyes got big, and he said, "Harley is dead?"

Zak replied, "Yes, the rogue alien thought he knew something about the formula, and when he found that he didn't, the alien killed him."

"He and his henchmen were returning from an attack on the Carver Brothers the night you took shots at them. The alien believes the Carvers know something about the water and algae formula and where it originates. I interrupted them from killing the Carver Brothers that night. The alien has vowed to kill anyone that gets in his way to find the formula, but I'm trying to catch and kill him before he kills more people."

Brumley asked, "So, are the Carver brothers still alive?" Zak said, "Yes, but only because I heard the shots at the Carver's house the night of the attack. I helped the Carvers fight the aliens off, and they abandoned their attack. But believe me, they will be back after the Carvers, and I told them that information, but they think they can fight the alien themselves. But they can't."

Zak said, "Mr. Brumley if you know something about that life extension formula, you need to tell me now so I can try to protect you from the alien killing you." Brumley took a deep breath and said, "No, I don't know anything." Zak shook his head and said, "I know you know something about it; how else could your dog look like it hasn't even been touched after it was shot? You had to have something that saved its life." He was shocked Zak would know about the life-saving substance but still refused to share any information with Zak. Zak said, "Ok, I wish you luck. You'll need it when that alien comes after you too."

Chapter 26 - The Safe Room

"I'm tired…I'm taking a few days off and going back to Julie and Christopher so I can relax," Zak said while standing and sitting on the edge of the military metal desk in Captain Hiller's office. "I'm not saying I'm dropping the case. I just need a brief break because I can't get anywhere with those people there in Arkansas," Zak added.

Hiller walked around the desk and sat in his desk chair, leaning back and intertwining his hands behind his head. The captain responded, "No sweat Zak. Besides, DeSoto might be holed up somewhere deep, even back in his dimension. Yes, take a few and then meet me here again at the base, and we'll see Brumley together about the salve and this elixir or whatever he calls the stuff."

"It's all tied to the source of the water like it's a youth serum or healer. I've heard it mentioned as an Algae, like a growth back in those mountains in Arkansas, near that town of Caddo Gap," Zak said. "Caddo Gap, can't get much more rural than that," Hiller mused. "Yes, but it's beautiful there, incredibly, and the people are amazing, almost youthful in their nature," Zak added. "You sure it wasn't because they were all loaded on the Carver brother's whiskey?" Hiller answered back with a half-smile. Zak smiled back, "No, not the whiskey, just exuberant, something I don't know. Anyway, so you're good for a few days while I'm home?" "Sure, now get out of here. Tell Julie hello for me," the captain said.

"Right on, can I catch a ride to Lilliwaup?" Zak asked. "We'll get you there. See you, Sargent," Hiller said. "Yes, Sir," Zak's said as he stood and gave a half salute, then walked out of the captain's office and headed toward the carpool and his ride.

DeSoto and his two comrades had parked a mile from Zak and Julie's Mountain home and hidden in the thick forest. He insisted they park deep into the woods, camouflage their vehicle, and then walk the mile to the house. Once they reached it, they would surprise Zak and his wife and kill him there, along with his wife. "Siratchik, I remember hearing there being a young boy in the house too," Roalm said. "Their son, we'll deal with that when it comes up," DeSoto answered.

The air was excellent, and the walk felt refreshing as the three walked toward the farmhouse, and the walk itself was heightened more so by their extra senses. They were hyper-alert and highly cautious. The terrain was ascending and descending in parts, then opened to a small valley that had an opening that emptied into an area that lay a well laid out farm, picturesque in its setting.

DeSoto and his two-henchman sat on a nearby ridge looking down on the home; DeSoto looked up to the failing sun and waited for it to be overtaken by night, knowing that this evening, this small part of humanity would not sleep in peace.

The sun began to move over the mountain's crest and set off a purple-orange hue that cast long shadows on the trees lining the hill. The evening was a light grey luminance that hung on steady before beginning to fade.

As the sun set, a greyish military sedan drove through the pass onto the farm road and stopped at the house's driveway. DeSoto could see the driver and the passenger exit the vehicle and recognized the passenger as Zak Thomas.

Moving over to his second henchman, DeSoto whispered to him to quickly go down the hill to the road and intercept the driver. He explained the rest of his plan to his henchman. He handed him the imaginator device and told him to hurry down the hill.

As DeSoto watched Zak Thomas and the other man speak to each other, he glanced down the direction of his accomplice and could see he was entirely out of sight and probably near the road. He then moved toward Roalm and motioned him toward the right side of the mountain to come down and circle to the back of the property and the house.

When Zak saw Julie and Christopher, his heart soared, and he had the biggest smile come across his face as they all embraced near the front door, Zak held on for the longest time, and then, Christopher began to sing a song, "She be comin round the mountain when she comes," he sang a few times then said, "Hi daddy." Zak knelt, picked him up, hugged him, and then said, "Hi," looking at both Julie and Christopher with a big smile and kissing them.

Zak set his bag down near the door when they entered the house. Julie blurted out, "I made us all a big late dinner," and smiled broadly. "Me too," Christopher added.

Just as Zak started toward the kitchen to see the great-smelling feast, a car horn beeped as it drove toward the driveway. Zak opened his front door and saw it was his military driver in the base vehicle in which he had just arrived after it had turned around after dropping Zak off and leaving.

Zak looked back at Julie, who had a little surprised look. "Stay inside, please." Zak said," I'll see what the driver needs," he added. Julie nodded as she stood near the kitchen entry.

As Zak stepped out of his front door, he peered out over the mountains to the left of the farm and then scanned the hills to the front, and as his eyes came forward to the vehicle, he calmly reached around to the small of his back to feel the small subcompact Colt - 45 pistol holstered there. He knew something was afoul.

"Hi again, Sargent," the driver said. Zak, seeing the driver was the same person who had driven him from Seattle, felt safe in the slight intrusion but was puzzled. "How can I help you, Corporal? Did you forget something?" Zak asked. "I think I did, Sargent," the Corporal said as he started to exit the vehicle and walk toward Zak.

"Well, first, let me ask you," Zak said as he stared at the soldier walking toward him. Is it you, or is it me?" Zak asked. "What?" The soldier said as he stopped and looked at Zak, puzzled.
"Is it you, or is it me?" Zak asked again. "It's me!" the soldier said with a small laugh and confusion in his voice.

Zak looked back to his shut front door and quickly turned back to the driver while reaching for his holstered forty-five and, bringing it around, shot the driver in the forehead with the Colt 45 pistol and blew out the back of the driver's head. Then stepping forward to stand over his driver with his forty-five still in his hand and aimed down at the man, lying on the ground dead, was the face of someone completely different.

Then stepping closer, he looked at the man and recognized him as one of the same aggressors in the room with DeSoto, who tried to kill him in his hotel room in Redding.

Suddenly shots rang out and pelted the ground and body in front of Zak. The darkness of the evening now fully descended upon the farm, making it difficult for DeSoto to get a good shooting position on Zak. At the moment that Roalm joined DeSoto, Zak was able to dash back into the house and grab Julie and Christopher. "I have to get you two to the safe room," Zak shouted. "You killed that man; wasn't he the one that drove you here?" Julie asked, frightened. "Yes, I did. When I stood in front of our house after he first dropped me off, we talked about our enemies' technology and how they can cloak themselves; remember how you and I talked about them?"

Zak hurriedly asked as they ran down the house's hall. "Yes," Julie answered, keeping pace with Zak. "Well, I told the driver a little about our enemy's technology and told him that if I saw him again for any reason, I would ask him a code question: IS IT YOU OR IS IT ME? His answer would be neither. The driver, when he returned, couldn't answer the question, and I had just talked to him about it before he left, and I knew he was an imposter," Zak said as they came to the wall containing the safe room and started punching in the numbered codes to open it. "But you shot him dead. Couldn't you have taken him prisoner?" Julie asked frantically."

"Honey, these people don't take prisoners. Their killers and his buddies are here too. It's DeSoto," Zak exclaimed as he pulled the safe room door open, "The alien murderer you've been trying to stop?" Julie asked, even more frightened. "Yes," Zak shouted, hearing pounding on the house's side door and the crashing sound of the front door exploding. "Now, keep you and Christopher in this room, don't leave for anything. Once the door locks, keep it locked. Please don't open it for any reason. An automatic call is made to The Agency once the door gets activated, and they'll be on their way as fast as they get the alarm. Now get in the room," Zak yelled, starting to close the door. "Zak, don't leave us," Julie screamed. Please, Zak, don't leave us," she screamed again, tears running down her face.

Zak stopped pushing the doors, looked into Julie's eyes, and felt intense love and protection. Then he glanced to his left and could hear the thunderous footsteps of two people quickly running nearer. At the last moment, Zak ducked through the door and, slamming it shut, heard the tight connection seal airtight.

Seeing Julie and Christopher were ok, he reached for the secure telephone on the wall, spoke the code words, and described the circumstances. The dispatcher assured him help was already on the way. As Zak placed the telephone on its cradle, an impact of immense magnitude hit the safe room door, and Zak recognized the sound as a round from an anti-tank rocket launcher fired at the door. But the room was constructed from thick metal sheets and withstood the blast.

"Can this room take that kind of bombardment?" Julie asked, looking around the room and holding Christopher tight. It should stand against most any onslaught." Zak said, looking up at the ceiling area.

Julie stood to grab a flashlight on the wall shelf. The second blast reverberated through the room and the room door held, but an oxygen canister large and heavy tore loose from the wall and tumbled to the floor, not before causing a glancing blow to Julie's head and throwing her across the room.

As the sound and rumble died down, Zak looked around the room and saw Christopher untouched but Julie lying on the room's floor, a red and bleeding gash on the right side of her head. She was unmoving.

Zak ran to Julie, picked her up in his arms, and held her. He could see she was still breathing and alive. Zak called Christopher, crying and shaking, over to him and hugged the boy while loud pounding was happening on the room's door.

Within a moment's notice, all sounds stopped, and a brilliant high pitch sound filled the room. Then all was silent save for a voice that filled the room. It was a voice he recognized.

"Zak, it's me, Rykert.

Chapter 27 – Zak goes to see Brumley

Zak wasn't sure if it was Rykert or DeSoto trying to trick him. He said, "Are you, my guardian angel? Rykert said, "A friend." Zak then knew it was Rykert and opened the door to see his old friend staring him in the face and smiling. He said, "Is DeSoto gone?" Rykert replied, "Yes, my comrades and I scared them off. That was a couple of rough wallops you took there, Zak." Zak replied, "Yes, it was. My ears are still ringing."

Zak had some urgency in his voice as he replied, "I have a problem here, Rykert, Julie has been hurt, and I can't wake her up." The two carried her out of the metal room and laid her on the couch. Zak then returned and got Christopher, who was crying and brought him to be by his mother's side. Rykert found a towel and wrapped it around Julie's head to stop the bleeding. Zak did his best to calm Christopher and tell him his mother would be ok, but he was scared and kept crying.

About forty minutes later, an evacuation helicopter landed in the front yard of their house. Zak went out on the porch, yelled, and motioned for them to send the paramedics in as soon as possible. Two of the paramedics grabbed their equipment and headed inside the house. They immediately started attending to Julie's head wound, but they couldn't get her to wake up.

One of the paramedics told Zak it looked like she had a severe concussion, but they needed to get her to the hospital to run a C-scan on her head. They brought in the metal table and quickly strapped her down for the ride to the hospital. Zak told Rykert, Christopher, and I will take the chopper back with her and meet up with you at the hospital. Rykert said, "Sounds good, Zak. See you there."

Zak had Christopher in his arms as he shut the doors to the house, ran, and jumped on the chopper. He was talking to Christopher and telling him his mom would be okay, although he wasn't sure. On the way to the hospital, Zak called his sister to see if she could get Christopher for a few days while Julie was in the hospital. Zak knew he would have to devote his time to being by Julie's side while she was there.

When Julie was unloaded from the helicopter and sent to the emergency room, Rykert was already at the hospital. He stayed by Zak's side the entire time the hospital ran tests on Julie. Zak's sister and daughter arrived at the hospital to pick up Christopher, taking a load off Zak's mind. He knew his niece would be a great comfort to Christopher. He told his sister he would come by in a few days to pick him up and let her know how Julie was doing.

When he had a minute to get his mind off Christopher and Julie, Zak said to Rykert, "I'm sure glad to see you, my friend, but what are you doing here?" Rykert said, "We have been getting reports about one of our citizens and a couple of his cohorts that had decided to leave our dimension and search for the riches of the eternal life substance that's found here on Earth. Our people control the substance he is searching for, but that guy wants complete control of our special formula. He is obsessed with having it for himself to get rich and gain fame." "Zak replied, "I know; I've been tracking him for a few months, trying to stop him. He's already killed several innocent people with this foolish quest. I killed one of his accomplices before they attacked us at my house."

Rykert replied, "Yes, we found out about his exploits recently, so two of my associates and I were sent here to find this fugitive calling himself DeSoto and his accomplices and return them to our dimension for discipline." Zak said, "I don't think they will go with you willingly." Rykert replied, "Then we will use deadly force."

"While you are here in the hospital with Julie, we'll start searching for them and make sure they don't come here," Rykert said. Zak replied, "Thank you, Rykert. That takes a load off my mind. I don't need them coming here and trying to kill us." Rykert replied, "I won't let that happen to you, Zak. We will find them and take care of the problem." Zak told Rykert that he would be great, go ahead and take care of the problem, and then let me know what happens. Rykert wished Zak luck and told him he would check back with him in a few days. Zak thanked him for being there for him and Julie.

They had Julie in a medically induced coma with tubes sticking out of her body. The doctor came out of the emergency room and talked to Zak. He shook Zak's hand and said, "Hi Zak, I'm Dr. Nassar. "We're not sure what will happen with her right now, but we are still running more tests to determine the extent of her head injury. Her brain had been starting to swell, and we had to relieve the pressure, so I put a drain tube in the back of her head to relieve the pressure. That will take care of that problem, but she took a severe blow to the head. She has one of those head injuries that may take time to heal. But Zak, I have to be honest with you. She could have permanent brain damage if she wakes up from this." Zak thanked him for his help and turned to hide the tears coming from his eyes. He was now blaming himself for this happening to Julie.

Zak spent the next few days in a restless spirit. He was angry with DeSoto, but the more he thought about it, the more he believed he needed to get his hands on some of that salve from Crawford Brumley. He wanted to try and give some of the substance to Julie and see if it would help. Her lying there in a vegetative state made him realize it might be her only resort. He called Hiller and arranged for the military to give him a ride down to Caddo Gap. Hiller said, "Ok, Zak, not sure why you're going there with Julie in her condition, but you got it, buddy."

Early in the morning of the third day of Julie's being in the hospital, Zak was picked up at the parking lot by a helicopter. He had the pilot fly him to the end of the road east of Caddo Gap. Once there, he told the pilot to wait for him. Zak said, "I have to hike up to this place and talk to a guy that lives a little further up in those hills." The pilot said, "No problem, Zak, I'll be here waiting for you to return."

Zak jumped off the chopper and jogged the dirt trail toward Crawford Brumley's house. He could feel the sense of urgency in every step he took. When he got there, he received the familiar welcome he had gotten before from the dogs until Crawford came outside and called them off.

When Crawford saw Zak, he said, "I didn't think I'd be seeing you again in these parts so soon." Zak replied, "Yeah, I know. It wasn't my intention." Crawford could hear some panic in Zak's voice and said, "What can I do for you, Zak? You seem distressed?" Zak said, "Yes, I am. I have a huge problem. My wife has been seriously hurt. Remember that rogue alien I told you about when I last saw you?" Crawford replied, "Yes, I remember." Zak said, "Well, he and two of his henchmen came to my house a few days ago to try and kill my wife and me. They tried to blow up a metal room my wife, son, and I had to hide in to keep from getting killed by them. While inside the protective room, my wife suffered a severe head injury, and I'm unsure if she will live. She is in a coma at the hospital. I didn't know who else to turn to for help, so I came here to see you." Crawford replied, "Me, what can I do to help her."

Zak said, "Don't get mad at me, but I know you have the salve that can help heal her if you would be willing to share just a small amount with me. You have reasons for keeping this substance for yourself, but as I told you last time, I want to try and help protect you and keep the alien from killing you. That alien is so desperate to find what he wants that he has been trying to stop me from killing him.

At first, Crawford got angry that Zak had asked him such a massive favor regarding the salve and its healing powers as he said, "Look, Zak, if that is true, you have to realize that I gave my word to a race of people that I swore I would never share their secret with anybody." Zak replied, "I know Crawford, I don't want the secret, and I'm not even asking you to tell me where it's located. I'm just trying to save my wife's life, and I think the salve will do that for her."

Crawford was hesitant at first as he slowly said, "I don't even know if that stuff will save her life, Zak. I've never had a chance to try it on myself or another person." Zak said, "It worked on your dog; that's how I knew you had the substance. Your dog would never have healed as fast as it did without the salve, and you know that is true." Crawford raised his eyebrows and looked at Zak as he replied, "Yes, it worked on him. Maybe it will work for your wife, but I can't guarantee it will. I guess you could take some of it and give it a try. After all, I'm not giving away any of its secrets."

He immediately got up, went into his house, and was in there a few minutes before coming outside. He was carrying a small metal container, and inside lay some of the green salve and a canteen filled with water from the source. He said, "Zak, I'm giving this to you to try and salve your wife. Give her the salve and the water in this canteen that comes from the water source. Give them to her together. But you have to promise me you will never tell anyone where you got the salve or the water." Zak stuck the can in his pocket, took the canteen, and said, "Thank you, Mr. Brumley. I promise your secret is safe with me. I hope it works to save her life." He thanked Crawford and quickly said his goodbyes.

Zak was out of breath when he returned to the helicopter from jogging down the trail. The pilot was patiently waiting for him when he got there. He thanked the pilot for waiting for him, and they soon sped back to the hospital. During the flight, Zak was nervous and anxious to arrive.

Once he got inside the hospital, he went to Julie's bed and sat with her. He waited until the nurses weren't in the room with her when he pulled the metal container out of his pocket. He took a plastic spoon, scooped out a teaspoon of the salve, opened Julie's mouth, and stuck it inside. He poured several teaspoons of water from the canteen into her mouth to wash the salve down to keep her from choking. She involuntarily swallowed what Zak gave her.

Zak ensured she didn't spit the salve out as he sat down in his chair. He held Julie's hand and watched her for the rest of the evening. Zak fell asleep in the chair, and a nurse brought him a blanket to throw over himself. He spent the entire next day and night with her, and not much visually had changed.

Zak was tired as he settled back in the chair next to Julie's bed and held her hand. He said a prayer for her and then slipped into a deep sleep. His mind was filled with thoughts of DeSoto coming after him, Julie, and Christopher. But in his dream, none of them were lucky to get away.

DeSoto walked into their house with his henchman and the Ion weapons fired from the time the door flung open. They were shooting everything in sight until they learned that Zak, Julie, and Christopher had taken protection in the metal room. Once they were outside the room, DeSoto and his henchman began firing heavy weapons at the room until it started to come apart. DeSoto pulled Julie and Christopher out of the room and began torturing Julie. That was when Zak began yelling, "No, no, I will kill you, DeSoto."

It was at that moment when Julie woke up from her coma. She was frightened as she squeezed Zak's hand and said, "Wake up, Zak, wake up." Not responding, she gripped his hand tighter and shook him before he awoke from the dream.

The first thing Julie said to Zak was, "Where is Christopher? Is he alright? Did he get hurt?" Zak replied, "No, he didn't get hurt. He is fine and with my sister. She took him home with her until you feel better and can come home."

Zak never had problems speaking, but he was elated that she was awake, and the salve and the sources water had worked. He stumbled with some of the things he was trying to say because he was so happy.

Julie asked, "What happened? I don't remember anything after we entered the metal room. How did I get here in this hospital." Zak took some time and explained everything that had happened.

Julie said, "What are all these tubes and lines coming out of me?" Zak said, "Well, you had a pretty bad bump on your head, and you even had a tube in your head to relieve the pressure from your brain swelling. Zak bent her a little forward, and even the hole where the tube had been inserted was closed. He said, "Everyone was worried about you and that you might not wake up because you've been in a coma for five days." He gave Julie a big hug and a kiss and held her tight as he told her he loved her.

Later, when the doctors came in to check on her, they couldn't believe the miraculous recovery Julie had made. They ran all the tests for a couple more days, and her tests were all negative for everything, so the doctor released her from the hospital so she could go home.

Zak and Julie arranged with his sister to stay with them for a while. At least until their house was fully repaired and there was no more threat of DeSoto attacking them again.

Zak quietly closed his eyes when he was alone and thanked Crawford Brumley.

Chapter 28 – Rykert goes after DeSoto

Rykert stood in Zak's sister's living room with Zak. He could see his friend's pain and despair had abated. Rykert said, "Stay and continue to comfort Julie." Zak turned and looked at her through the glass slider doors. She was sitting on a patio chair outside with Zak's sister with a knitted blanket covering her lap. Zak could see that Julie was smiling as she talked to his sister, and he said, "I need to be here for Julie and Christopher for a few more days.

Rykert said, "We'll pursue and bring in DeSoto and his remaining accomplice and prosecute them for their crimes," Zak replied, "You have to find them first. Where would you even begin to search?"

"When my companions and I came to your home, it was because I had an immense feeling that you needed my help. Our bond goes way beyond the dangers we've faced together on your missions in the past. We are friends. Regarding how to track Siratchik or DeSoto, when we checked your home's property while your advance rescue team tended to you and your family, we found plasmatic residue left by three individuals of Nether origin. We also found the corporals body, who was your original driver. You killed the Nether that had unfortunately taken the

Corporal's life and transformed into his likeness, leaving two others. The two others who had forced themselves into your home and attacked your family left plenty of fingerprint and DNA samples scattered throughout your home. We know who they are. Allow us to get them."

"You remember you said that the key to this mission may be in the state of Arkansas?" Rykert said. "Yes," Zak replied, "We think those two are headed back. We have a trace on the plasmatic residue, and it may point us in their direction," Rykert said, smiling. "Outstanding buddy, go get them, Zak said."

"I'll check back in with you when I can," Rykert said as he extended his right hand to Zak. Zak clasping Rykert's hand shook it firmly and nodded his consent, and then Rykert turned and walked out of the room.

It was three o'clock in the morning in Las Vegas, Nevada when DeSoto's fast-moving craft shot across the sky below the radar. At the helm was DeSoto as he looked for the empty Swamp Meet location on the outskirts of town. Finding its place, he quickly sat the craft between two vacant buildings. After checking to ensure nobody was watching their descent, he and his comrade exited the craft and headed for the central part of town.

A huge sign flashed neon lighting. The sign read: WHAT DO YOU DO WHEN YOU'VE CONQUERED THE EARTH, and then the name of the famous pop star flashed across the screen.

DeSoto looked up at the grand marquis above the imposing casino hotel. "Bullshit!" DeSoto said as he spat out the word. "What did you say, Siratchik? Roalm asked, picking up his bag and walking toward the entryway to the hotel. "Nothing!" DeSoto said, glancing up to the marquis once again before entering.

"Want tickets to the show?" The hotel's door attendant yelled out toward them. "Fuck no!" DeSoto snarled. "No thanks, buddy, we're just passing through," Roalm said to the man as the two passed by him.

"You've got to chill, Siratchik, I know you're pissed about missing Zak Thomas, but we're still in the running. Just chill out with these people while we're here." Roalm implored DeSoto. "What the hell do you know how I feel? Just mind your shit," DeSoto said, highly agitated.

DeSoto wanted to get a basic room at the huge hotel and got lost in the multitude of crowds that flocked to the desert oasis. That way, they could be undetected and undeterred. He told Roalm, "Let's check in and get some sleep before I plan our next move. Roalm was good with that.

It was around noon when DeSoto and Roalm met up for lunch. DeSoto gave Roalm five thousand dollars and said, "Make this last a couple of days while we're here. Also, keep an eye out for suspicious individuals who may look like they are after us. We now have other Nethers after us, besides that guy Thomas."

They split up but kept an eye out for each other as they mingled in the crowd of people gambling to try and win their fortune. Roalm sat at one of the blackjack tables, pulled out his gambling money, and began playing. He stayed on the table for several hours as his money went up and back down again, but he stayed primarily even. DeSoto also played blackjack at one of the tables for several hours, and his luck was about the same as Roalm.

The winds that wisp the desert sands were beating hard on the cars that traveled in and out of the desert town. Rykert had set his craft down in a lonely and dark place in the desert. His four Nether companions continued walking as they were transported into a narrow alleyway on the outskirts of Las Vegas, oblivious to the medium-sized sandstorm their transported energy had generated.

Rykert gazed down at the heat displacement detector in his hand. All Nethers gave off a little higher body heat signature than humans, and Rykert had traced two such signatures here in this town.

When Rykert and the Nethers exited the alley, they were thrust into a myriad of lights and action so intense one of the Nethers gazing at the splendor said aloud, "Wow." Rykert just smiled as he continued to look down at the heat detector. "There appear to be two signatures indicative of our subjects in that direction," Rykert said, pointing his right palm to the left. "But honestly, there's a lot of high body heat being given off in this town, particularly in the hotel areas," he added. He then started walking in the direction of a large hotel with a large marquee.

Rykert and his Nether companions were armed with the Ion guns and could avoid being detected by U.S. technology. They had cash from previous missions, and Rykert split it between them and told his companions. "Let's try to get these two guys alone, so no other people have to die."

After several hours of gambling, Roalm decided he needed a break and headed to his room to get some rest. Before he took the elevator to his left, he saw a bathroom and decided to use it. Two of Rykert's companions who had spotted Roalm at the Blackjack table using their heat sensor and watched his movements followed him into the bathroom.

Once inside, they confronted him, and he wasn't willing to give up his freedom to go with them. One of the Nethers reached out to grab Roalm's arm, but Roalm lashed out and struck the Nether in the arm with a concealed knife.

A gunbattle broke out and lasted a few minutes before Roalm turned himself into a shadow, thinking he could hide from the Nethers. The two Nethers also turned themselves into shadow people and continued trying to stop Roalm. Not seeing him, they used their heat sensors to follow Roalm throughout the casino, occasionally firing shots at what they thought was him. Their Ion weapons blew holes in the casino walls as they tried to pinpoint Roalm's exact location. He was taking shots at what he thought were the two shadow figures following him.

The Casino security personnel were utterly shocked as they tried to follow the shots from the weapons but could not see anyone firing them. It wasn't long, and the entire casino was filled with security people trying to stop what was happening. They had all exits blocked, with nobody coming in or going out, except shadow people.

Roalm tried to get away as he walked past the security guards and exited the casino. Once outside, he began to run down the main street the Casino all faced. The Nethers also exited the casino and gave chase. While running, Roalm would occasionally turn around, looking back, and run into a few pedestrians and knock them down along the way. Not seeing anyone, they were shocked by what happened to them.

Roalm was heading toward Siratchik's craft, but he would stop after a few blocks and take blind shots in the direction where he thought the Nethers were. The Nethers continued their pursuit for several blocks until one of them started firing in the direction of Roalm to draw his fire. The other went a few blocks ahead, got in front of Roalm, and waited for him.

The Nether got an excellent heat reading on Roalm, and when he got closer and fired several shots at him. Roalm was still alive and firing back in the direction of the Nether, but now he was caught with one Nether in front of him and one behind him. The trailing Nether advanced and used the heat sensor to get a good read on Roalm and shot at him a few more times. At that point, Roalm was hit by one of the shots fired and lay dead on the sidewalk. Then he began to materialize from his shadow effect. After several minutes bystanders started approaching Roalm's body to see what had happened. The police were called, and sirens could be heard in the distance.

The two Nethers also materialized and met Rykert in the front of the hotel, standing under the large Marquee. "We were able to eliminate one of the criminals, Rykert. We tried, but there was no chance of apprehension."

Rykert said, "Siratchik has escaped. He immediately turned himself into a shadow person as soon as he realized what was happening with his ally. He must have known he was the next one we would go after. I couldn't pinpoint him exactly, but he left the Casino because he left all his casino chips on the table and quickly left.

Rykert said to his comrades, "Go retrieve the Nether's body.

When he got to his craft, DeSoto was angry and disappointed as he sped off alone in the direction of Arkansas to his next destination.

Rykert reached into his coat pocket and dialed Zak's cell phone number, and he reached Zak immediately. "Hello, Zak," he said. "How's Julie doing?" Rykert asked. "She's doing better and recovering amazingly. She is still a little tired and weak, but the doctors say she will fully recover. Thanks for asking. Anything new on your end?" Zak asked.

"We missed Siratchik here in Las Vegas. We did eliminate one of his henchmen, but I suspect Siratchik is long gone from this location," Rykert said. There was a long silent pause, then Rykert added, "I also suspect he may be headed to that small town in Arkansas you mentioned. Do you want us to go after him?"

"No! No, he's mine," Zak said emphatically. "I'll take care of him. But thank you and your guys, my friend, head home. I'll let you know if I need you further." "Very well, Zak, bye for now," Rykert said and began to walk in the direction of the alleyway and their way home.

Chapter 29 – DeSoto attacks Orville

DeSoto was angry that he was now left to pursue his goal alone of finding the water and algae. He was also now aware that the Nethers and Zak were after him. Regardless, he wouldn't let either squash his desire to squelch his obsession. The desire was so strong DeSoto couldn't stop himself. He would push on no matter what it would take or how many lives it would cost.

He believed the answer to him finding what he wanted was in the sole fate of Orville Carver. He was convinced the water he was looking for had something to do with the Carver brother's smooth whiskey. They didn't make any bones about it being the best whiskey in the Country to anyone.

Orville drank so much whiskey during the day that he stayed half-drunk most of the time. DeSoto believed Orville's inebriated condition would cause him to slip up and give away the whereabouts of their much-kept water secret. DeSoto knew he could get Orville to talk if he could get him alone and not kill him during the process.

It was starting to get dark when the house was set on fire. The blaze and smoke lit up the eastern part of the sky. It was the home of Charlie and Orville Carver. They had been hiding at their cousin Scottie's house for a few weeks before the fire was set. It wasn't long before Charlie and Orville discovered their family home was on fire. DeSoto became frustrated in not knowing where they were hiding. Hearing the news of their house on fire, they quickly made their way to the fire, but by the time they got there, the house was almost burned to the ground.

When they saw the fire, "Orville said, "Them son of bitches came back again, Charlie, and burned our damn house down. Just like they said they would." He had his rifle out and searched for the culprits that may have started the fire. He confronted some of his neighbors and said, "Did yuns see anybody trespassing around here before that fire was set?" Everyone said they had not seen anybody near the house or on the property.

Orville went over to Charlie and said, "This is some crazy ass bullshit, Charlie. They burned up everything we own." Charlie said, "That guy Zak, from Homeland Security, said they would come back and burn our house down, but we didn't believe him. He also said they would try to kill us.

We must keep our eyes open because that alien, or whatever he is, has it in for us, and he will try and kill us."

Orville whispered to Charlie, "Should we say to that guy where we get our water for our whiskey? I don't want to die because of that secret about the water." Charlie said, "Shut up, Orville, that kind of talk will surely get us killed if you're not careful. We got to spot that guy before he sees us and then blow his head off." Orville replied, "You don't have to worry about that. If I see him, he's a dead man."

Charlie and Orville sat on a couple of logs with their rifles raised toward the sky while watching the fire burn the house the rest of the way to the ground. All the neighbors and friends grew tired and left. They kept an eye out just in case DeSoto showed up to kill them. Around midnight, Charlie said, "Well, that about does it. Let's get going." Orville was still cursing under his breath as they made their way to the truck.

DeSoto had been watching Charlie and Orville from the woods safely away. While they were distracted from watching the fire, he returned to their truck and hid under the tarp in the truck's bed.

It was a bumpy ride as he lay perfectly still until Charlie pulled into their cousin Scottie's place and parked off to the side of the house. He and Orville went to the door, pushed it open, and stepped inside. Scottie was sitting on the couch and said, "Well, looks like those people did what they said they would do and burned your damn house down. We all better sleep with one eye open just in case they find this place and break in here to kill us. I don't want them burning this place down."

DeSoto jumped out of the truck, crept to the window, watched, and listened to what was happening inside. He got a good look at Scottie and, aiming his imaginator device, scanned a perfect image of him. He waited for a while and watched where Orville was sleeping. About an hour later, DeSoto cloaked himself to look like Scottie and stepped inside. He went into Orville's room, where he was sleeping. Once there, he said to Orville, "Hey, Orville, grab the keys to the truck and follow me." Orville didn't understand what was happening but immediately obeyed who he thought to be Scottie.

Once outside, DeSoto decloaked himself, grabbed Orville by the collar of his shirt, and threw him in Charlie's truck. He pointed his Ion gun at Orville as he said, "Ok, drive. I want you to take me to where you get your special water." Orville immediately went into a wild rage and began fighting DeSoto. He said, "Are you the fucker that burned our house down." DeSoto laughed and said, "Yes, I told you I would be back to burn it to the ground if you didn't give me what I wanted." Orville was no threat to DeSoto as he beat Orville nearly senselessly and then told him again to drive. He said, "You try something like that again, and I'll kill you the next time."

Orville started driving toward the spot in Buttermilk Creek, where they got their water. When they turned a sharp turn in the road, Orville jumped out of the truck and began to run. DeSoto was prepared for Orville's attempted escape and caught up with him and beat him again. Orville's face was covered in blood from the cuts above his eyes, cheeks, and lips. DeSoto grabbed him, threw him back in the truck, and said, "You are one crazy idiot. I guess you like pain." Orville said, "Why do you want to know so much about our water? It's just water?" DeSoto laughed and said, "It's not just water. It's much more than that to me." Orville said, "No man, it's just water, nothing else."

They finally made it to the Still close to Buttermilk Creek, and DeSoto recognized the place. He yelled, "You got to be kidding. I've been here before; this can't be where you get your water." He demanded Orville show him the pool of water from the Creek. Once there, DeSoto waded out to his knees, cupped the water in his hands, and drank a handful. He asked Orville, "Where does the source of this water come from?" Orville said, "I don't know, never been to the top. It's deeper in the Holler, in a cave near the waterfall. Orville didn't know the source's exact location but had a fair idea. One night in a drunken state, Crawford eluded the source's whereabouts to the brothers but quickly retracted his words and never spoke of it to them again. DeSoto went into a rage as he began to beat Orville some more. He said, "That's it, that's all you know?" Orville said, "What else is there to know? I just make whiskey, bro."

He beat Orville some more, kicked him five or six times, and left him by the Still to die. He took the truck and headed up the canyon as far as he could drive before running out of room to go any further. At this point, he had to abandon the truck and head by foot the rest of the way to the top.

When Charlie went into Orville's room to check on him, he found that Orville was gone. Going outside, Charlie also saw that he had taken the truck. He and Scottie immediately began driving around the hills, looking for Orville.

It took a few hours to find Orville, and he was almost beaten to death but alive. They immediately took him to the nearest hospital for treatment. Once Orville was cared for at the hospital, Charlie and Scottie returned to where they found Orville. They began searching up by the Still for his truck. Charlie believed that since Orville was found at the Still, the guy that burned their house down and beat Orville was the one that had done this. He believed his truck would be in that same general area.

Charlie followed the fresh tracks of the truck until they came to his truck parked a few miles up the path from the Still. When they found the truck, Charlie told Scottie, "You go back to town and tell the police what has happened and that I'm after the guy and going to kill him." Scottie replied, "I'll do it, Charlie. I hope you catch that piece of crap and put his lights out." Charlie armed himself with a rifle and a handgun and began following DeSoto's trail. DeSoto seemed to be following the creek further up the hills.

When Scottie returned to town, Zak had just pulled into town after hearing about Charlie and Orville's house being burned down. He heard Scottie tell the police what had happened to Orville. Zak told Scottie who he was and asked if he would take him to the spot where he dropped Charlie. Scottie agreed.

Charlie had a head start on Zak by a few hours, so Zak had to hustle to try and catch up with him. He wanted to catch him before he ran into DeSoto, and Desoto killed him. It was still dark when Zak finally caught up with Charlie. He was fighting, angry about what had happened to Orville, vowing to kill the person responsible.

Zak had to convince him the alien had weapons that could quickly kill him if he weren't careful in his search for DeSoto. Zak said, "We'll find him together."

Chapter 30 – Zak and DeSoto showdown

It was the early morning hours, and the waterfall cascaded over the edge of the green-sloped mountain in the dim light. The morning light had shifted and shone down on the valley below, illuminating the top part of the slope.

The entrance of the cave, covered by moss, tree branches, and ferns, was easily breached, but Zak was cautious. He knew the cunningness that DeSoto continuously displayed. On the other hand, Charlie was spurred on by his anger and passion, determined to reach his quarry before he could elude them further.

Zak and Charlie had followed the trail as they arrived while it was still dark and stood at the base and peered into the five-foot crevice where De Soto had escaped.

As the two leaned forward and worked their way through the narrow passage, they could see evidence of moss disturbance where a recent object or person pressed against it. The ground they walked on was wet and also showed signs of passage. Zak pulled his bright flashlight in front of him and matched Charlie's light illuminating the way.

The two men entered an expansive underground room surrounded in the sand, exposing a sandbar that emptied into a fast-rushing stream flowing through the cavern and under a massive mountain of rock.

Zak flashed his light around the open ground area and could see no movement or indication of DeSoto. To his left, Charlie motioned to what resembled a doorway built into the side of the rock. Zak walked toward the doorway while shifting his Ion pistol to his right hand. Charlie looked around again and slowly followed, tightly holding Orville's twelve-gauge shotgun with both hands in a ready position.

A five-foot entryway opened to a flat area eight feet in diameter. A fissure had split the earth, and a twelve-inch wide sliver showed down from the top of the slope and burned down the early morning light on a slab of rock, causing the small room to be somewhat lit up and specifically lit the rock slab that held a green body of algae that poured over the side into a pool of water that ran into a stream which poured under the rock and into the river on the other side of the rock wall.

Zak walked over to the algae and stood, fascinated by how it shimmered in the light. It reminded him of the story of the shimmering green substance Dr. Stanton had told him and Rykert about and its believed healing properties. "Could this be the same?" he thought. "Is this what caused the rumors and had created legends for centuries, the fountain of youth," as his eyes ran down to the pool of water at his feet. Zak kneeled on one knee and cupped the water in his right hand, "Is this what DeSoto has killed for?" he softly said out loud.

Suddenly, Charlie shouted behind him, "He's out there." Zak bolted for the doorway, with Charlie following close behind. As they came into the open area, Zak could see DeSoto standing near the river with a backpack on his left shoulder, and in his right hand, he held a plastic liter container with a patch of the algae in it, and it was filled to the brim with water from the pool.

DeSoto stood devilishly smiling, knowing he had been caught. The men could see he was readying himself to jump into the stream that flowed under the mountain and again make his escape. As he placed the liter container in the backpack, Zak shouted, "Stop if you want to live. Throw down the bag and put your hands behind your head." DeSoto's eyes darted around the cavern and then focused on Zak.

Stalling for his next move, DeSoto said, "Have you seen him?" "Who," Zak said. "Man," DeSoto replied. "You mean mankind?" Zak asked. "No!" "Man, the creator, De Soto fired back." "God," Zak nodded in understanding as he moved closer to DeSoto and, looking directly at him, asked, "Have you...seen him?" "No," DeSoto replied, "But I have been close," he added. "Interestingly, you Humans call yourself Man," he continued. "You would believe yourselves to be Gods. But you are only like Man, created in his image, like me, Man kind."

Zak thought it didn't sound like DeSoto as he said, "I don't know what you are, but you're not Mankind or Man or a God," Zak said as he lowered his eyes and then lifted them once again to gaze at DeSoto, he said, "You're evil." Zak said again, "Put your hands behind your head," as he started to remove a zip tie from his coat pocket." I'm taking you with me," he added. It was at that moment DeSoto made his next move.

Standing slightly behind Zak to the left with Orville's twelve-gauge shotgun, Charlie Carver raised it and aimed it at DeSoto. A blast rang out, hitting Desoto in the lower leg. As he struggled to stand on one leg, Zak once again said, "Give up, DeSoto." DeSoto tried to grab his Ion gun from its holster when a shot hit him again. It was in his right shoulder, and he could not grab his Ion gun. DeSoto was determined to fight even with two shots in his body. The next shot fired was when Zak shot him in the head, blowing the top portion off his head and spattering flesh and bones onto the rocks below DeSoto. The projectile's impact threw him into the stream and washed his body downstream and underneath the mountain.

Charlie said, "My brother is in the hospital because of that sumbitch, and all the people he's killed. We're better off without him. He was nothing but a mad dog. He needed to be put out of his misery." Zak stood confused. It all seemed too easy.

Zak walked over to the area where DeSoto had stood, with no blood or tissue on nearby rocks. Seeing that his body had washed away under the rock, Zak turned around and thought. "How could that be possible? Did he fool us again?"

Suddenly a loud explosion rocked the cavern and caused rock and dust to pour into the area where Zak and Charlie stood. Thrown to the ground, Zak lifted his head to see the entrance door to the algae pool had been partly destroyed and somewhat collapsed on itself. The rest of the cavern remained untouched and intact, aside from a lot of dust and rock rubble. Zak and Charlie quickly made their way out of the cavern and into the morning light.

"What the hell happened?" Charlie asked between coughs. Zak said, "DeSoto must have rigged the entry with explosives, probably trying to trap us inside," Charlie replied, "Well, it backfired on his ass."

That's when Zak knew that DeSoto was not dead. A frown crossed his face as he realized that DeSoto had used his GPS to set up a vivid life-like hologram of himself standing in the dark area. It was his identical image standing on the rock and talking, but it wasn't him. It was the hologram. DeSoto was hidden at the base of the entry to the cave.

Even the action where he disappeared into the river was all planned, just like DeSoto wanted it to look. It was the image that Charlie and Zak shot and not DeSoto. DeSoto believed he could get away with his plan once Zak thought he was dead.

Zak yelled out, "He did it again. Come on, Charlie, DeSoto is heading back to town." Charlie was confused as he said, "What are you talking about, Zak? We just killed him." Zak replied, "That wasn't him, he's still alive, and we have to stop him before he gets back to his craft. He thought his plan was working perfectly because he had had the water and algae in his backpack and headed down the mountain toward his craft. It was parked in the woods just outside Caddo Gap and not too far from the ashes of Charlie and Orville's burned home.

Zak was jogging ahead of Charlie and slowed up for Charlie to catch him. He said, "I'm going to run ahead of you and see if I can catch up to DeSoto and cut him off. I'll see you somewhere down by your truck." Charlie was already out of breath and slowing down as he said, "Ok, Zak, that sounds good. He still couldn't believe DeSoto was still alive."

As Zak made his way down the mountain, he thought, "I can't believe I fell for that trap of DeSoto's. He sure had me fooled." His knowledge of past experiences with how crafty DeSoto could be made him vigilant enough to realize DeSoto had tried to pull a trick on them.

A few hours down the mountain, Zak caught a glimpse of DeSoto walking briskly down the mountain path. Zak slowed to a fast walk to catch his breath and think about what he would do to stop DeSoto. Zak thought about his options and decided to speed up, circle in front of him, and catch him further down the path. He thought, "You can't trust this guy. He'll try everything to try and trick you." This experience reminded him of one of his last encounters with the vicious killer Shief, who hunted Zak in the Pacific Northwest. He, too, was crafty, but it was an inner evil demon that drove him to his destruction. Zak had to kill him on a lonely mountain trail.

Zak made it to an area about two hundred yards ahead of DeSoto. He was winded and gasping for air as he found a position just off the path and took cover. Zak only had to wait a few minutes when DeSoto came down the path toward where Zak was hiding. When he got within thirty yards of Zak, he stepped out in front of DeSoto with his Ion weapon drawn and aimed at DeSoto. He said, "Hold it right there, DeSoto. This is the end of it. There's no going any further. You've killed enough people."

DeSoto said, "You're a fool Agent if you think you can stop me. I've trekked all over this country and finally have what I've been searching for this entire time." Zak said, "Yeah, but look at the people you killed to get what you wanted." DeSoto said, "They were all just collateral damage, and if they would have given me what I asked for, maybe they would all still be alive."

Zak said, "You can throw that bag over your shoulder onto the ground, and I'll take you prisoner, and I will let you live. If not, you will receive the same judgment you gave the ones you killed. You can die here on this lonely trail or go back and face your consequences." DeSoto replied, "I'm not giving up this bag, and I'm not going to be a prisoner to you or anyone. Why do you think you can stop me? What is it that you want, Zak? Recognition, fame? You can't be doing this for your country?"

At that moment, DeSoto started trying to turn himself into a shadow figure, and Zak recognized what he was doing. Zak didn't hesitate and instantly fired his weapon at DeSoto's chest, and the Ion weapons round caught DeSoto in the upper chest and ripped a hole through his heart. As he lay there on the ground taking his last breath, Zak shot another round through DeSoto's forehead. He then took the back pact from DeSoto's body with the water and algae and said, "You should have listened to me, DeSoto. You'd still be alive."

Zak waited for Charlie to catch up to him. When Charlie saw DeSoto's dead body lying on the ground, he said, "This is crazy stuff. I was sure he was already dead back up yonder." Zak said, "This guy has been a hard one to kill, Charlie. He was like a chameleon and could disappear before your eyes, and he almost did it again."

Zak called Hiller and told him he had killed DeSoto and that he could send a team to retrieve his body.

Chapter 31 – Going Home

When Captain Hiller arrived with his crew to retrieve DeSoto's body, he saw Zak sitting on an old, worn-looking park bench in front of the Carver's burnt-out house. Zak was tired and worn out.

Exiting from the back seat of his government SUV and walking up to Zak, Hiller wanted to say, "You look like shit," but seeing the look in Zak's eyes and the deep emotion there, he merely said, "You look tired," and sat down on the bench opposite Zak. Continuing to look up at the captain as Hiller sat down. Zak said, "Deeply," as he continued to look at the captain.

"So, it's over?" Hiller asked, looking at Zak. "Yes, it's over. This one was tough; I wasn't sure we would get this guy because he was elusive and crafty. But he's dead. We can all go home," Zak answered.

"You're heading back to the farm?" The captain asked. "Back to the farm, to my family, to my real life," Zak said, brushing his hair once again for any particles of rock and sand.

"Good luck, buddy, see you on the next one," Hiller said, standing and prepared to walk to his government SUV. "If there is a next one," Zak said, smiling briefly at Hiller, who turned and walked to his vehicle.

Zak watched the two vehicles pull out of the driveway and make their way to the old road heading out of town, carrying DeSoto's body. Then Zak stood, collected his gear, and readied himself for the journey home.

As the SUV passed the trees lining the road out of town, their leaves beginning to lightly brown in the turning season, Hiller could see the small rolling hills with the occasional farm dotting the countryside, with the deep forest in the distance. He whispered, "With all the monsters in this world, there will be a next one, Zak."

Poem

Written by Ron L. Carter and H.R. Carter
Dedicated to the people of Caddo Gap.

"I'm going back to Caddo Gap."

Someday I'm going to go back
To a place, they call Caddo Gap

In the hills near Hot Springs
Where people don't sweat the small things

The women are so beautiful and shy
And they don't ever ask you why

Their lips are soft and sleek
Like the water in Buttermilk Creek

Some say you can lose your life in Bear Den Hollow
Just take my word and don't dare follow

Life is so peaceful from Round Top Mountain
You might think you found the fountain

It's where de Soto took his last stand
And the Indians won back their land

If you ever go looking for the Ridge
You can't miss old Swinging Bridge

It's where men are men and boys are boys
They carry their guns instead of toys

They love their country and will fight to defend
Even if their life comes to an end

Raccoons hunt way into the night
With Red Tick hounds and a flashlight

It makes you crave that simple life
With a little house and an Arkansas wife

Sources of Information
Wikipedia – The Free Encyclopedia

Special Thanks
We want to thank Laura Shinn for developing the book's
cover:  laurashinn.author@gmail.com
http://laurashinn.yolasite.com

Other Books by Ron L. Carter
Twenty-One Months – non-fiction
From the Darkness of my Mind – fiction
Unearthly Realms – fiction
The American Terrorist – A Grandfather's Revenge -
fiction
The American Terrorist – The Revenge Continues - fiction
Night Crawlers – fiction
Night Crawlers – Reign of Terror – fiction
Accidental Soldiers – fiction
Love me now, don't wait – Poetry

Other Books by Ron L. Carter and H.R. Carter
In Defense of Mankind - fiction
Zak Thomas – The Monster Hunter - fiction

Made in the USA
Middletown, DE
07 October 2022

12037901R00097